Catch Me

A DEER CREEK FALLS NOVEL ~ BOOK ONE

ELLIE RHODES

DOUBLE TAKE PUBLISHING

Cover Design by: https://www.madcatdesigns.net

ACKNOWLEDGMENTS

Many thanks to our editor Jessica Peirce, our author friends, and friends who support and encourage our author career – you know who you are!

Heartfelt love to our awesome, supportive husbands.

CHAPTER ONE

*P*aige Turner loved her early morning walks to work. Manhattan came alive with the scent of fresh-baked bread and ground espresso. As she pressed her shoulder to the heavy brass door of Cagney and Cahill Publishing, Paige tucked a strand of her wavy blonde locks behind her ear and hurried to the coffee cart inside. "Good morning, Charlie."

"How's the latest book? Is it a real *page-turner*?" His brows bobbed over their ongoing joke. Only Charlie and Paige's best friend, Chloe, could get away with the punny name jokes; with Charlie, it was their thing.

Paige rolled her eyes. Her mother had thought it amusing to name her Paige, since her grandpa owned a bookstore. A bookstore in the small town her mother couldn't wait to flee from. The place that helped shape Paige's love for words.

"How's your pops doing?" Charlie poured milk into a stain-less-steel pitcher and placed it under the steamer.

Paige raised her voice over the hiss of the steaming milk. "I talked to him this morning. He's out of the hospital and having a hard time getting around. I have a few things to finish up at the office today, and then my flight leaves tonight. He's going to need someone to run the bookstore while he recovers."

"You're a good kid." Charlie poured the steamed milk into a cup. "The land of 10,000 lakes, that's gotta be somethin' to see."

"It is beautiful."

"I bet." He topped off her drink with an ample serving of whipped cream and handed it to her. "Here you go, a tall double dark mocha with a splash of mint for my favorite editor."

She inhaled the rich scent, took a sip, and sighed. *So good.*

"The best coffee in the city, Charlie. Oh, I almost forgot." Paige fiddled with the clasp of the worn brown leather satchel stretched across her chest and flipped the flap open. She reached inside, pulled out a book, and handed it to Charlie. "This is for Henrietta. I guarantee she'll love it. L.C. Brooks is an up-and-coming author I highly recommend. It's the first title in a series. The third book hits the shelves in July."

July first to be exact, and every time she thought of the deadline looming over her, she had to fight off a panic attack. Paige had counted on using her well-deserved vacation time to finish the book, but family came first, and it was time to return home. Besides, she hadn't visited in years and she missed her grandpa. She wasn't like her mother, who couldn't wait to leave the small town she grew up in for the big city, but the big cities were where the jobs were. Paige breathed deep and tried to calm her mind.

Charlie accepted the book and ran his hand over the cover. She loved people who still appreciated paperbacks: the smooth touch, the inky smell . . . physical books were the lifeblood of her grandfather's business. Charlie studied the cover then quickly flipped it over and skimmed the back.

"*Catch Me*. It's about baseball? She's gonna love it. Heck, maybe I'll even like it," he said with a wink.

"You might. Give it a try." Paige knew Charlie's wife loved

both baseball and romance. He always showed Paige the latest selfies taken at Yankee Stadium. They talked about baseball often, she a Boston fan, he a die-hard Yankees fan. Every day, he wore the same black baseball cap turned backward over his short-cropped salt-and-pepper hair.

Paige dropped a few bills into the glass tip jar. "Alright Charlie, have a good one. I'll see you in July."

Charlie nodded. "You bet. Enjoy."

She stepped out of the elevator on the fourth floor and made her way through the maze of cubicles. She liked the quiet time before most of her coworkers started their day.

Paige set her bag and coffee on her desk. She couldn't help the snort of humor that slipped out as she picked up a crocheted Babe the Blue Ox that had been left for her.

"Good morning, sunshine." Henry, her cubemate, smiled at her over the padded half-wall.

She held up Babe. "This is great, Henry. Thank you, I love it."

"I had extra yarn. And I wore this for you." He adjusted his buffalo-plaid bow tie.

Paige moved her fingers over the soft yarn of the ox while a smile tugged at her lips over Paul Bunyan's famous bright blue sidekick. It was both a silly and thoughtful reminder of home. "How very lumberjack of you."

Henry, with his stylish blond hair and boyish good looks, would be adorable in any bow tie. Before he and Michael had become a couple, he had dated more cute guys than Paige had.

"I thought it fitting since you're leaving me for two months to go live in the land of big, burly men in checkered shirts."

"I'll be back in New York for the gala. If you run into any problems, don't hesitate to call me."

"Don't give the gala another thought. Michael has everything under control."

Lately her cubicle felt as if it were closing in on her like a padded cell. But because of Henry and his good-natured fun, she wasn't in a straitjacket yet. She needed this vacation, even if it was a working one.

"When do you fly the coop?"

"Noon. I hope."

"You must be excited Allen's tour brings him to Minneapolis. Will he be spending time in Deer Creek Falls with you?"

"No." She and Allen were done spending time together. Paige turned on her computer. "I have no desire to see him anytime soon."

"Let me guess. You told him you published your own books and he insisted he couldn't be with anyone who wasn't *traditionally published*."

Paige lowered her voice as more of her colleagues filed into the office. "No. I didn't tell him and he didn't break up with me. I ended it."

Henry glanced around the room and waved to a newcomer. "Good. I didn't like him much anyway."

"*Really*. I couldn't tell."

"He's an egotistical ass. Good riddance. Tell me this: if Margo decides to sign you, will you tell Allen you're a"—Henry made air quotes—"*published author*?"

"It doesn't matter much anymore, now does it?"

Paige glanced at the glass-enclosed office of the acquisitions editor.

"Margo should be here soon," Henry said. "Any word yet on your manuscript?"

"No, I hope to catch her before she runs off to a meeting."

Henry sat back down, disappearing behind the wall.

Paige placed Babe by her mouse pad and restacked her Post-it notes. She set her out-of-office reply and dusted off her desk, waiting for Margo to arrive.

"Psst." Henry popped back up, his wide-eyed expression setting off her alarm bells. "Allen just walked in the door."

"What?"

Paige panicked, grabbed her briefcase off her desk, crouched low, and crawled around the cubicle wall and under Henry's desk. Yes, she was a coward. She'd broken up with him by text message. If she had written him a letter, he would have found fault in her writing and corrected the damn thing.

"He really is ruggedly handsome," Henry observed. "Too bad he's such a jerk . . . Paige? Where did you go?"

Paige yanked at Henry's pant leg and he let out a high-pitched yelp. Shit. She shouldn't have done that. He always startled easily.

Henry peered under his desk. "What are you doing under there?"

She held a finger to her lips. "Shhhh."

Henry popped back up. "Sorry everyone, I thought I saw a mouse."

There were collective gasps from their co-workers.

"Donna, hon. You have three-inch heels on and you're standing on a chair on wheels. Get down off there before you break your neck. It was a false alarm. No mouse."

"Are you sure it wasn't a mouse?" Donna asked.

"Yes, I'm sure. It was a toy I crocheted for my cat. It fell off my desk and it startled me."

The office was filled with groans and the sound of chairs being pushed back in place.

Paige bit down on her lip as Allen approached Henry.

"Henry! Have you seen Paige?"

"Allen, I thought you were on tour," Henry responded.

"I had to take a later flight. Where's Paige?"

"I believe she's on her way to Bora Bora."

"Bora Bora?"

What was Henry thinking? Like Allen would believe she was in Bora Bora.

"Well, I'm not sure. She had a few weeks' vacation saved up and mentioned she needed to clear her head. Maybe she said she was going to see her grand—oww!"

"Where?"

"Oww-ahu. Yeah. Oahu. She's meeting her friends and maybe her grandpa or something. I'm not sure. I was distracted by this adorable text from Michael."

Paige placed a hand over her mouth so she wouldn't laugh out loud.

"He is so sweet. He sent me a picture of a—"

"Never mind. Margo must know." The disgust dripped from Allen's voice.

"Margo hasn't arrived yet. I'm happy to keep you company until she does."

Paige wanted to cheer. Henry had a way of bringing Allen's true character out into the open. Allen hated when Henry brought up his partner, and he sure didn't want to hang out with Henry any longer than he had to. Paige heard Allen mumble something.

Henry ducked under his desk. "He's gone, little mouse."

As ladylike as possible, she crawled out from under Henry's desk. "Thank you, Henry, I owe you one."

Thirty minutes later, Henry looked over their shared wall. "Margo is here. Go get 'em, tiger."

Paige ran her hands down her grey dress pants, palms sweaty, and headed toward Margo's office. She knocked twice on the open door. "Margo, do you have a minute?"

"A minute, yes. Come in."

"I know you're busy. I wanted to check if you've had time to look at my manuscript."

She stood in front of Margo's desk and waited for her to get settled.

"Have a seat." Margo gestured to the chair in front of her desk.

Margo removed Paige's manuscript from under a pile of others and placed it in front of her. Folding her hands on top of the papers, she leaned forward.

"Here's the thing, Paige. Although it's a decent story, there just isn't a big enough audience for sports romance. Cagney and Cahill have only a limited number of spots for romance novels and I can't recommend yours. I'm sorry." Margo handed the manuscript back to her, and Paige stood.

Her stomach clenched. "I understand." She had hoped with the sales of her first two books, she could convince Margo she was worth taking on as a client.

"How's your grandfather doing? You leave tonight, right?"

Paige swallowed past the lump in her throat. "He was released from the hospital and yes, my flight leaves tonight."

Margo leaned back in her chair. "Try to enjoy yourself, Paige. We'll see you after the fourth."

And just like that, Paige was dismissed. She closed the door softly behind her and took a few cleansing breaths. Chin held high, she walked back to her cubicle.

Paige felt a new respect for all authors who submitted their manuscripts and were rejected. She understood how hard it was to land a publishing contract, but she'd thought by writing two successful books, having an established media presence, and working for a publisher, she'd have an advantage. *I guess not.*

Henry was sitting in her chair when she returned. "It went that well, huh?"

She tossed her manuscript on top of her leather satchel. "I don't get it. I've sold over twenty thousand copies of my first two books and have a social media following of over three thousand people."

Henry stood and hugged her. "Hey, her loss. I don't know why you need Cagney and Cahill. Keep doing what you're doing and they'll be begging you for your books." Henry winked. "Then, when they realize your brilliance, turn them down."

"I know, but—"

"Listen Paige, you know more about the publishing world than most writers. You've published two books on your own already and you've made a decent income from them. Trust yourself."

Henry was right; she did know a lot about publishing and selling books. She'd hired an awesome and experienced cover artist who loved cats as much as she did, and who'd created stunning covers and formatted her books. Henry was her second set of editing eyes, and she had beta readers who offered both expertise and constructive criticism.

"You're right. Thanks, Henry."

"So . . . are you going to tell anyone you're an author?"

"Chloe knows." Paige smirked.

"I would assume so, but what about your grandpa? How do you think Abe will feel if he finds out from someone else? Isn't he selling your books?"

Henry and her grandpa, both quirky in their own ways, had hit it off the moment they met the previous year when Abe came to visit. Although she knew Henry had a point, she wasn't ready to reveal herself. Not to her grandpa, not to anyone from her small town. The thing about small towns was that everyone knew everyone and their business.

Paige chewed on her lower lip. "Well, yes, because I recommended them." She smiled. "I can't exactly tell him. He'd figure out I based my hero on Ethan Reynolds, and I'd rather be saved from the embarrassment."

"It's going to come out eventually."

"What good is it to have a pen name if you can't separate your work and private life? Besides, I'm only going to be home for a couple of months. I doubt the subject will come up."

"Keep telling yourself that."

CHAPTER TWO

*D*eer Creek Falls, Minnesota . . .

After a long day of installing docks, Ethan Reynolds walked into his favorite local hangout, the Eagle's Nest, to watch the Twins play the Mariners.

For years, only a select group of locals frequented the old establishment, until a new owner renovated it, hired a chef who created gourmet burgers, and established happy hours and game nights.

Ethan spotted his oldest brother, Roman, at the bar. In their family of six siblings, they were the two brothers who looked most alike: over six feet tall and with similar features, except for Roman's smattering of gray along his temples and throughout his close-cut beard.

"Hey, man," Ethan said. He settled onto the bar stool next to Roman. Roman had been running Reynolds and Sons, their parents' landscaping business, for the past seventeen years, since their father died.

"I figured you'd stop in. Did you get a chance to install Abe's dock?"

"Just finished." Ethan nodded to the wide-screen television that hung on the wall. "How are they doing?"

"The Twins' new catcher is looking good."

The bartender approached and set a coaster on the high-gloss bar. "What can I get you?"

"Tall amber." Ethan swiped a French fry off Roman's plate. Roman was having his usual, a bacon bleu burger basket. "And I'll have what he's having."

"You got it."

The Twins hit a two-run homer. A cheer went up from the handful of Wednesday-night patrons.

"The way they're looking this year, they'll be beating a lot of records," Ethan said. The bartender set down the tall amber and turned to help another customer.

"Are the girls at Mom's?" Ethan asked. Roman's ex-wife had long ago decided she preferred the single life, leaving Roman to raise their twin daughters on his own. Ethan didn't know how his brother juggled the family business and two busy adolescents.

"Nope. They're at a birthday party. A sleepover."

"You're kidding. The girls are out of the house and you're sitting at a bar watching a ball game?"

"I'm not you. The ladies aren't exactly falling at my feet."

Ethan inclined his head toward a table to their left. "That woman has been eyeing you since I arrived."

"Hardly. Her attention only turned our way when you got here. She's looking at you, little brother." Roman took another bite of his burger and continued to watch the game.

"I'm not looking for a relationship." Ethan said.

"Who says anything about a relationship?" Roman smirked, but Ethan knew Roman was just as much a relationship guy as he was.

"Here's to bachelorhood." Ethan held up his glass, and his gaze rested once again on the television.

He and Roman had become closer since he'd moved back to Minnesota. Although the nearest they came to talking about relationships had just occurred, they'd both been burned before. Unfortunately, his nieces also paid the price for their mother's fickleness. Ethan was glad he hadn't had kids before his own breakup, or he'd be in the same boat as Roman.

The bartender set Ethan's dinner in front of him. "Can I get you anything else?"

"No. Looks good." Ethan ate a fry and watched the Twins retake the field.

Roman's phone pinged. He glanced at the notification, and his fingers flew over his screen. He looked at Ethan. "You bought Turner Books?"

"How do you know that?"

Roman held up his phone. "It's on the Town Talk app."

"Let me see." Ethan grabbed the phone out of his brother's hand. *Ethan Reynolds buys Turner Books.* He set Roman's phone down on the bar. "That's not entirely true. I don't know how you can stand having a gossip app on your phone."

"Care to set the record straight?"

"I bought the building, not the bookstore. The bookstore is still Abe's."

"Why?"

Ethan shrugged. "It's an investment."

Roman picked up his phone and started typing.

"What are you writing?"

After Roman finished typing, he handed his phone back to Ethan. *Ethan bought the building, not the bookstore.* "Town Talk is far from the tabloids you appeared in. Yes, it's gossip, I suppose, but it's not meant to hurt. We try to get our facts straight. Plus, the only people who have this app and post on it are the people of this town, and in case you haven't noticed, they idolize you, Mr. Gold Glove Winner."

"Yeah, yeah, but I still refuse to download it. I didn't take you for a Town Talk user."

"Well, if you had twin daughters close to puberty, you'd download it too."

A man wearing a reflective vest and steel-toed boots approached Roman and patted him on the back.

"Hey, Wes," Roman said.

"This your brother?" Wes said to Roman.

"Yes."

"Nice to meet you," Ethan said. He shook the man's hand.

"Wes is one of our plow drivers in the winter," Roman explained.

"So, you come home to run the family business?" Wes asked Ethan.

"Nope, just helping out where I can."

"That catcher the Red Sox got to replace you has nothing on you. I'm going to miss watching you behind the plate. But I guess it's pretty nice to be retired in your thirties."

Ethan shrugged as if the easy comment didn't have teeth. Talk of his retirement tended to gnaw at him. "Yeah, it can be."

Roman stood up and tossed some cash on the bar. "I'll catch you later, Wes. Long day tomorrow."

"Catch ya later." Wes moved toward a table with other highway workers.

Ethan stood too, and tossed a bill on the bar, silently thanking Roman. He understood why people envied his retirement at an early age, but the comment always stung.

He'd devoted his early years to playing baseball and was grateful for the successful career he'd had, but being away from family for the majority of his twelve years in the major leagues had taken its toll on his relationships and his family. He also missed playing ball and being around his teammates, many whom he considered his brothers too.

Ethan followed Roman outside, and they stopped in front of Ethan's truck. "Sorry about Wes," Roman said.

"No biggie. I'm used to the comments."

"Doesn't mean they don't sting though, right? So, buying real estate is in your future?"

"I don't know. Helping out a friend, that's all."

Roman patted him on the back. "I'm proud of you, little brother."

Ethan hadn't wanted anyone to know, but who was he kidding? Small towns were the pinnacle of gossip. He groaned as he lifted himself into his truck.

Ethan had the radio tuned to a local station. The host was taking requests for songs and calls from people expressing their love for their soul mates. Frustrated at his lack of companionship —unless he considered Fenway, his tabby cat, company—he reached over and pushed the button to change the station, opting to listen to the rest of the game on his way home.

He got caught up in the play-by-play, and before he knew it, he was in his driveway, shifting his truck into park. He stepped out and his knee buckled. Ethan grabbed the truck door to keep himself from falling onto his face. Mentally he was still in his twenties at the peak of his career, but physically there were days he felt sixty. He limped into his house, grabbed a beer from the fridge, and collapsed into his leather recliner. Fenway jumped onto his lap and head-butted him, wanting attention. He scratched the cat under his chin to make him purr, breaking the silence.

He couldn't remember a time growing up when his childhood home was silent. Screen doors slamming, his siblings bickering and his grandma yelling to wash up for dinner. He missed those days.

Keeping busy maintained his sanity. The nights he wasn't eating dinner at his mom's, he would grill a steak or burger and watch a game. Any game. It didn't matter. Tomorrow was another day. He was fine. Everything was fine.

ETHAN GOT AN EARLY START the next morning, the sun barely breaking the horizon. One of his jobs working for his family's business was to fill in wherever he was needed. This morning he watered the plants lining Main Street. The baskets, a colorful mix of wave petunias, hung from ornate iron streetlamps. The large concrete planters in front of the businesses were filled with a mixture of pansies, daisies, assorted greenery, and fresh-cut branches.

He breathed in the cool spring air. He'd been away from his hometown during fishing opener for more years than he could count. If he were still playing in the major leagues, the baseball season would be in full swing. Back when he was on the road and missing home, he'd go to the ballpark and watch the grounds crew work. He'd breathe in the scent of freshly mowed grass and listen to the *shhhh-tik-tik-tik* of the sprinklers. Now he was home, and a restlessness was setting in—was he cut out for retirement?

Ethan had just finished watering the sidewalk planters when a hooded figure ran into the dark alley where the wispy dawn light had yet to reach. The hair on the back of Ethan's neck stood up. His intuition said this wasn't simply an early riser out for their morning jog. There was something about the hooded figure dashing through the shadows that had his body humming on full alert. Armed with only a penlight, Ethan crept along the rough brick wall of Turner Books to the back alley. He shot off a quick text to his friend Nick, the interim sheriff with the Deer Creek Falls police department. He knew Nick would back him up if he could.

Ethan crept closer. When he peeked around the corner of the

bookstore, the hooded figure was crouched down, picking up rocks and flipping them over. Definitely weird behavior for the average morning jogger, especially since Ethan knew Abe kept a key hidden by the back door.

If word had gotten around—which no doubt it had—that Abe Turner was recovering at home from a fractured leg, a burglar might take the opportunity to rob him blind.

Not giving it another thought, Ethan ran up and pressed his flashlight to the stranger's back. "Hold it right there!"

PAIGE DID what her self-defense classes had trained her to do; she turned on her aggressor, pivoted on her left leg and kicked with her right. She hit her attacker in the chest and he stumbled back with a surprised grunt. Her hood slipped off and she stood facing him, hands up, protecting herself. Her heart beat so fast she thought it would burst from her chest.

Recognition clicked, and Paige dropped her hands to her sides. Of all the people . . . she was staring at Ethan Reynolds, a frown etched on his face. Ethan who, with his ruffled brown hair, hazel eyes, and slight stubble, in combination with his performance on the ball field, was no stranger to magazine covers. Ethan, who she'd only seen from a distance, usually the third-base line since the night he'd saved her all those years ago. Her heart fluttered.

She flashed back to the moment like it was yesterday.

The Bakers were hosting the senior class party at their estate on Balsam Lake, and for Paige, going to the party was starting to feel like a mistake. Ronnie Baker was spoiled and a notorious bad boy. All the girls fawned over him, but not Paige. She had tutored him in English as a favor to her teacher when Ronnie needed to increase his grades to play football. When they were alone, he flirted with her, but she never returned his advances. The popular kids in school ignored her, so she knew his flirtations were just for show.

That night, Ronnie was drunk and surrounded by his football team as he motioned her over to them. Paige held a beer she had no intention of drinking; it made her look cooler than she felt, and it gave her something to hold on to. The uneasy feeling creeping up her spine gave her pause, but she walked up to the group with as much confidence as she could.

When she joined the group, Ronnie asked if they could talk alone. She'd been alone with him many times when she tutored him so, leaving the ear-splitting music behind, she followed him out onto the deck. Ronnie swayed on his feet. His eyes roamed over her body, stopping on her breasts. "You were my favorite tutor." He ran his hand along her arm.

Paige's adrenaline spiked, and with sweaty palms, she reached for the door. "Glad I could help." But she was too slow.

Ronnie pulled her to him, his lips smashing onto hers. She struggled to push him off, but he was too strong.

Suddenly, Ronnie was pulled away from her. Ethan had come to her rescue.

Paige shook her head to try and dispel the memories invading her brain and returned to the present. She pulled her earbuds out. "Did you seriously just try to hold me up with a flashlight?"

"Did you *seriously* turn around with something pressed to your back? What if it was a gun? If it helps, I thought you were a guy." Ethan said.

"Wow. What I think is that I almost knocked you on your ass." With hands on hips she looked at a stunned Ethan Reynolds. Was he surprised to see her? With his brows scrunched and head tilted slightly to the side, she wasn't sure what he was thinking.

She motioned toward the penlight in his hand. "That's a little small for a gun, or maybe that's all you're packing?" She fought the urge to let her gaze drop down his body and refused to blush over her sarcastic reply but dammit, he'd scared her. The last thing she'd suspected her trip to the bookstore would result in was being held up by Ethan Reynolds. Not that she would mind being held up *against* Ethan, as in being pressed against a wall with . . . she really needed to pull herself together. Wait. Had he just insulted her?

Her teenage crush, the man she'd fashioned the hero after in her first book, thought she was a guy? She worked hard for her figure, with endless trips to the gym, kickboxing classes, and running in Central Park. Was she as self-conscious about her looks as the next woman? Of course! But she knew her body was lean, not broad. Toned. So why did he think she was a guy? And here she'd been looking forward to Rosie's strawberry-rhubarb pie. Great. Just great.

They both turned toward the police car racing down the alley. Ethan grabbed her arm and held on tight.

"What do you think you're doing?" Paige said.

"You're not going anywhere." Flashing red and blue lights reflected off the brick walls. Ethan waved to the officer as he climbed out of his cruiser with a hand hovering over his weapon.

Paige turned to Ethan and tried to pull from his grasp. "You called the police?"

"Technically, I texted them."

As the officer approached, she recognized him as Chloe's brother. "Hi, Nick. I heard you were the new sheriff in town. Congratulations."

Ethan looked at her and then to Nick. *Interesting,* Paige thought. *He has no idea who I am.*

"Good to see you, Paige. I heard you were going to be in town for a few weeks. Chloe mentioned you were meeting for lunch at Rosie's today."

Ethan let go of her arm, turned, and stared. "Paige? Paige Turner?"

"Yes, Ethan. It's been a long time. You look the same, but then again, I've seen you in the news."

"I'm sorry. I . . ." Ethan glanced between her and her family's bookstore. The shop she had every right to enter.

She pinched her lips together, but there was no stopping her grin over his mistake and his obvious discomfort.

Nick patted Ethan on the back. "Alright, if you don't need my help apprehending a burglar, I'll leave you two alone."

"Thanks Nick, sorry about pulling you away from keeping the citizens safe," Ethan said, his voice dripping with sarcasm.

Nick shook his head and waved as he walked back to his cruiser, then climbed in and drove away.

Boy, had she missed these small-town, friendly jibes between friends. And after all these years, it seemed Nick and Ethan remained close. They'd both grown up to be ridiculously handsome. Both muscular, oozing testosterone, but well-mannered and humble. Nothing like the men in suits she encountered daily. *Sigh.*

"You okay?"

She hadn't meant to sigh out loud. Oops. "Yep. Fine."

"So, what were you going to do with the rock you were holding?"

"Gramps said I would find the spare key under a rock. I didn't think there'd be so many."

The corner of Ethan's mouth tipped up, revealing his dimple. *So sexy.*

Ethan walked to the other side of the door and picked up a stone turtle, sliding its shell to the side and pulling out the key. "Here you go."

"How did you know where it was?"

Ethan shrugged, put the turtle back together, and placed it back in the pile of rocks. "It's always the turtle."

She stepped closer and took the key from his hand, her fingers grazing Ethan's palm. "Thanks."

Ethan smelled of spring and fresh earth. Paige inhaled his scent, and then felt the heat rise when he smiled, clearly realizing what she had done. Darn, she shouldn't have leaned into it. Apparently embarrassing herself around him was her thing, like high school all over again. *Ugh.*

ETHAN WATCHED Paige shuffle her feet, her cheeks taking on a rosy glow as if maybe she found him a little bit attractive. She'd definitely changed—from the shy, awkward girl he knew in high school to a sexy spitfire with ninja skills. She'd gotten rid of the geeky glasses she used to wear. He hoped she still had them. She could pull off the sexy librarian.

He needed to remind himself Paige Turner was off-limits. No matter how attracted he was to her. Last he heard she lived in New York, and Nick had said she'd only be around for a few weeks. She'd probably be gone as soon as Abe could get back to running the bookstore.

CHAPTER THREE

*P*aige entered through the back door of Turner Books, and the sweet and musky smell of old books brought back a flood of memories. Every day, she'd walk home from school and head straight for her grandpa's office to fill him in on her day. Then she'd spend the remainder of the afternoon propped against one of the bookshelves, reading or doing homework. God, she missed this place.

When she stepped through the door of Abe's office, she thought maybe someone *had* burglarized the place. Piles of papers littered the old wooden desk, cardboard boxes filled with books lined the walls, and scrunched-up sheets of paper spilled over the sides of the metal trash can. The carpet needed cleaning and had unraveled at the seams. Pictures, some of her when she was little and some of Abe smiling next to now-famous authors who'd visited the store, hung crooked on the walls. She'd been gone too long.

Paige removed her sweatshirt, readjusted her ponytail, and went to work. The closet no longer had a door, and the shelves were bursting with books and supplies. She found a sleeve of trash bags, took one out, and began to sort through papers. When had Abe become so messy? When she was home a few years earlier, it wasn't this bad, was it? She would have noticed, wouldn't she?

Paige selected her fitness playlist and got to work. A little while later, her phone vibrated with an incoming text, and she pulled it from the blue paisley armband Abe had given her for Christmas. "I know how much you love to run in Central Park, and I'd feel better if you had your phone," he'd told her. Her grandpa made her laugh; of course she carried her phone.

Need milk, oatmeal, and bananas. Please, read Abe's text.

Paige responded, *You bet. See you after lunch.*

Thanks. Love you, sweet pea.

She sent a red heart emoji.

Paige stacked brightly colored sticky notes into a neat pile. She couldn't help her obsessive organizational skills, especially when it came to the office supplies she loved so much. For her, stocking up at a back-to-school sale was like being a kid in a candy store.

A leather-bound ledger caught her eye. Paige caressed the soft leather and opened it. She flipped through a few pages, noting a number of transactions that caused her concern. Abe had recorded several large monetary transfers to her mother, at least one per month for the last six months, and there were a few past-due utility bills. Not wanting to deal with it just then, Paige decided she'd take the book home to delve deeper into the store's financial situation.

She could feel her blood pressure rising. Since she did her best cleaning when angry, the office would no doubt be spic-and-span when finished. She and Abe were going to talk, and she knew the perfect time to do so. Paige got back to work and tried hard not to dwell on what she'd learned. Her grandpa was still sending money to her mother.

A few hours had passed by the time she tied the last trash bag. She stood and admired her work. The office was now organized and clean, and the only thing she needed to do was vacuum.

Paige started through the long, narrow building toward the front of the store, flipping light switches on as she went. Some of the fluorescent lights flickered, but many of them buzzed and only half lit. She scanned the store and wondered if it had always looked so run-down.

As she passed one of the bookshelves, Paige ran her hand over a row of books the way she had when she was small. Before closing the shop for the day, she and her grandpa would stand on opposite ends of a bookshelf, her forefinger resting on a book. Paige would walk slowly toward him, dragging her finger along the spines. When her grandpa said "stop," she'd pull the book her finger stopped on from the shelf and flip it open to a random page. She'd read a passage out loud until she got to a name. The name became a character in the bedtime story her grandpa would tell when he tucked her in at night.

At the sound of a noise Paige couldn't quite place, her attention snapped back to the present. She moved toward the front door in time to see something furry run along the wall, then change direction and run toward her. She screamed and took off for the bathroom, slamming the door behind her. It wasn't like she had never seen a squirrel before, but they'd always been outside —where they belonged.

She felt a little ridiculous, but it was exceptionally large for a gray squirrel, at least the size of a Chihuahua, with a big, flicky tail and nut-crunching teeth. Paige pulled up her big-girl panties, took a deep breath, turned the doorknob and pulled.

The knob came off in her hand.

She was stuck in the bathroom. At least the squirrel wasn't trapped inside with her. Thank God for small favors. Determined to free herself, she pushed the knob back into place, causing the other end of the doorknob to fall into the hallway. This new setback was made obvious by the heavy clunk of vintage metal making a *thunk* against the thin carpeting. Useless knob in hand, she bent down and peeked through the hole. Dumb squirrel. He looked angry. He stood on his hind legs and chattered at her. It seemed he was yelling at her for being stupid. She didn't disagree. "Hey buddy, do you think you can pick up the knob and put it back in the door?" Okay, she was losing it. Who talked to a squirrel? Good thing her phone was still on her arm. She sent a quick text to Chloe.

Hey, I'm stuck in the store.

Three blinking dots appeared. Bless her heart, she was already texting back.

Np, I'll save you a seat.

Paige was going to be more than a little late for lunch if she couldn't escape.

No, I'm stuck. Help! Back door is unlocked. I'm locked in the bathroom and there is a rodent keeping me hostage.

Brt, Chloe responded.

Paige hated text talk; why couldn't people use complete sentences? Although truth be told, she did like emojis.

She figured she might as well clean the bathroom while being held hostage. The cabinet under the sink held everything she needed, so she scrubbed the sink, the toilet, and the grout. What was taking Chloe so long?

Finally, there were approaching footsteps, and not of the squirrel variety. These were followed by a knock on the door. "Paige?"

The voice was distinctly masculine. Not Chloe. Wonderful. She'd know that voice anywhere. "Ethan? Where's Chloe?"

"She couldn't get away from the store. Customers. So, you're stuck in the bathroom?"

"*Ding, ding, ding*! Give the man a prize." Paige heard a chuckle. She took a deep breath. "Did you see the squirrel?"

"Nope. No squirrel out here." Ethan put the knob back in place. "Okay, thread the knob on your side back on."

With a little jiggle, the door opened. Ethan stood in front of her with his arms crossed and a smirk on his face. She couldn't help herself; Paige perused his muscular legs and arms. Such a nice sight to see. The smirk remained. What an ego. But yet, so amazing.

"Shit!" The gray rodent ran between Ethan's legs, making him jump.

"Told you there was a squirrel in here." She smiled.

"I'll set a live trap and figure out how he got in," Ethan said.

"I'll take care of it," Paige said.

"It's not a problem. It's my responsibility now that I own the building. Plus, the festival committee is meeting here tomorrow morning, and I don't need anyone else locking themselves in the bathroom."

"Technically, I didn't lock myself in the bathroom. The doorknob broke. Wait—back up. You own *this* building? Since when?"

"Abe didn't tell you?"

"No, he did not. And there's a meeting here tomorrow? I'm driving Abe to his doctor's appointment tomorrow."

"I know. Abe already asked me to open the store."

"Great. Okay. Well . . . I have to go. I'm meeting Chloe for lunch. Um . . . you know where the key is."

What the heck was going on? Ethan bought the building? Did he own the store, too? *Abe, you have some splainin' to do!*

❦

LOCATED on the corner of Main Street and Lake Street in a historic three-story brick building painted ivory with black trim, Rosie's Café was an institution in Deer Creek Falls. Black awnings shielded large display windows flanking each side of the entrance. Half-round arched windows with decorative trim showcased the apartments above.

Paige pushed open the door to the tantalizing aromas of home cooking. The curious patrons stopped eating and turned in their seats.

Rosie shrieked, "Paige! Well, I'll be. If it isn't Paige Turner back from the big city. It's so nice to see you." Rosie had been one of Paige's grandmother's best friends. Paige hugged her. She hadn't changed a bit. Her voice carried in a sing-song melody after years as a professional opera singer. Sporting short silver hair and still soft around the middle, she wore one of her customary chunky jeweled necklaces, a black uniform, and colorful clogs. Her style spilled over into the décor of the café, with the booths covered in a glossy red vinyl and the counter stools a mixture of bright colors. Framed opera posters adorned the walls.

"It's nice to see you too, Rosie."

"Honey, you are too skinny. I've already set aside a piece of your favorite rhubarb pie."

Paige placed a hand on her stomach. "I've been dreaming about your pie."

Chloe waved from a back booth. Paige had known Chloe since the first day of kindergarten, when Chloe grabbed her hand and told her they'd be best friends forever.

"Go on back and I'll be right there to take your order." Rosie hurried off.

Chloe jumped up and hugged her. "I've missed you."

Paige always admired Chloe's classic, no-nonsense style. She wore a U2 *Joshua Tree* concert tee, gray-washed jeans, and violet

Converse Chuck Taylors. Her messy auburn bob and brown eyes complemented her flawless complexion.

Paige laughed. "We talk almost daily. You look great."

She slid into the booth, leaned close, and teasingly chastised Chloe. "I can't believe you sent Ethan." She was still feeling fluttery about running into him twice in one day. There was something about having a hot man call the cops on you then later free you from a bathroom that could have a girl feeling off-balance.

"I was busy, and he was in the shop." Chloe shrugged.

Rosie approached and slid a piece of pie in front of Paige. "I know how much you enjoy dessert first."

"Thank you, Rosie, you're the best." She'd need to run every morning if she planned on indulging in dessert while she was home.

"I understand you're working on the store before you re-open."

"I started early and accomplished quite a bit. I hope to open in a few days."

"That's great, Paige. I know your grandpa appreciates you coming home to help." With order pad in hand, Rosie asked, "Now, what can I get the two of you for lunch?"

Her grandpa was slowing down. That realization scared Paige to her core.

"I know what I want," Chloe said.

"Me too."

They ordered the same dish they had when they came to Rosie's as kids: a hot beef sandwich with mashed potatoes and brown gravy.

"Did you know Ethan bought Grandpa's building?" Paige whispered.

"Not until I saw it on Town Talk." Chloe leaned closer. "Do you know why?"

"I don't know, but I have a feeling I know why Abe needed

the money. I'll get the truth out of him when I drive him to his doctor's appointment tomorrow."

"Perfect, trap him in the car where he can't escape."

"You know it."

CHAPTER FOUR

*T*he jingle of the front door sounded, and a chorus of voices filled Turner Books. The Deer Creek Falls Festival Committee had arrived. Ethan's grandmother Elsie led the group and went by the philosophy that if you were right on time, you were late. They were ten minutes early. Since his grandmother had lived with him most of his life, Ethan had been raised with the same principles and knew he needed to be at the bookstore in plenty of time to set up for the meeting.

Ethan met the group at the door and caught a box before it slipped out of his grandmother's arms.

"Good catch. I'm glad to see you're still putting those skills to use." Elsie reached up on her tiptoes and placed a kiss on his cheek.

"At Abe's suggestion, I've set up a place for you in the back room."

"Thank you, dear." She patted him on the forearm and headed toward the back.

A parade of women followed his grandmother through the store like chicks being led by a mother hen.

The women took charge and placed carafes of coffee, napkins, silverware, dessert plates, and a few white bakery boxes on the table. Ethan hoped one of the bakery boxes held Rosie's famous strawberry-rhubarb pie.

"Where's Paige?" Rosie asked him.

It was unusual to gather in the bookstore without a Turner present, but Ethan was happy to help the family out. "She drove Abe to his doctor's appointment this morning."

The women all talked at once, sounding like a flock of geese flying south for the winter.

Elsie pulled a gavel from her oversized purse and banged it on the table, making her sister Emma jump. As former mayor of Deer Creek Falls, Ethan's grandmother took her role seriously as head of the DCF Festival Committee.

"Where did you get that?" Emma asked.

"It was a retirement gift." Elsie waved the gavel and bathed her audience with a smug smile.

Emma rolled her eyes. "Lucky us."

Ethan loved his grandmother and her twin sister, his great-aunt Emma. They kept him and his siblings entertained.

Everyone took their seats, and Chloe poured herself a cup of coffee and passed the carafe.

"First," Elsie began, "I'd like to thank Ethan for joining the committee while Abe recovers. As you all know, and I'm reiterating for Ethan's sake, we've formed this committee because the number of tourists has declined over the last few years with the long winters and ice out after fishing opener. Our neighboring communities have pathetic Fourth of July festivities, and our goal is to remind people what makes our town special." She looked to the group seated around the table. "After our last meeting, each person had a task to complete."

Rosie piped up. "Ruth couldn't make the meeting, but she wanted everyone to know that the Deer Creek Lodge will be hosting the beer garden. Our local hottie, Garrett Reid, will be pouring samples of his latest brew, Loon Call Lager."

"You're talking about my brother," Chloe said, taking offense at the term "hottie."

Rosie, with a flip of her hand, waved off Chloe's comment. "I talked to my niece, and she volunteered to drive her food truck here from St. Paul. She makes a mean pulled pork." Rosie breathed deep. "I can smell it now."

"Maybe we could get a few more food trucks?" Elsie said.

"Good idea. I can check with my niece."

"Great."

Ethan's stomach growled, and he realized he hadn't eaten breakfast. Chloe must have heard the rumble, because she passed him a bakery box. He selected a glazed donut. Chloe placed a white napkin in front of him. "Thanks," he said.

Alexis Welby, the local contractor, addressed the group. "The Eagle's Nest has booked the Roadhouse Romp for their street dance."

"Oh, how wonderful. They can really shake it," Emma said, moving to a soundless beat.

Ethan thought Emma was a hoot. Though identical, the twin sisters were anything but in personality. They dressed differently, each with her own unique style. Emma had never given up her hippie look. Her short white hair always had a different colored streak—this week's color was purple—and she wore Birkenstocks and long, flowing, patterned skirts. Her earrings dangled from multiple holes in her ears, and her eclectic selection of bracelets jangled when she talked with her hands.

Elsie wouldn't be caught dead with a streak of color in her hair and wore conservative and classic clothing. Emma was very much the artist, Elsie the businesswoman. Emma, an art teacher at the high school for many years, loved to travel during the summer and had visited Ethan in Boston a few years back. Emma was the life of the party when she hung out with him and his teammates after a game. His teammates commented that they wished they had such a cool great-aunt.

"Sorry I'm late, everyone." Ethan's mother, Linnie, rushed into the back room and pulled out a chair. Ethan wasn't surprised his mother was late. She had too many irons in the fire, as his grandma would say. His mother still helped Roman run the landscape business and helped his sister Maggie run the resort, which their paternal grandfather had left to Maggie in his will.

"I was helping Maggie welcome her first guest to the cabins. The three cabins she has ready are all rented out," Linnie announced.

"That's wonderful! I'm so proud of her." Emma clapped her hands together.

"I'm glad you were able to help," Elsie said. "We've just started reporting on our assignments. Did you get a chance to talk to Zeke?"

Zeke, Ethan's youngest brother, an electrician by day, playboy by night, was also a volunteer firefighter, and Ethan guessed the turnout gear helped him land the ladies.

"Yes, and the fire department has agreed to set up their dunk tank. They want to do a Christmas in July theme to raise money for the Secret Santa fund." Linnie said. The Deer Creek Lodge had held a Christmas event every year since Ethan could remember, including organizing and distributing presents for Secret Santa.

A chorus of oohs and aahs filled the silence.

"I think we need more ways to entice people to come," Chloe said.

"You're right, we could use some other activities. Any ideas?" Elsie asked.

"Ohhh, I have a great idea," Emma said. "The fire department should sell calendars."

The women's chatter intensified, and the ideas were spiraling out of control like a fighter jet plummeting to the ground. The gavel banged and everyone quieted down.

At first Ethan had thought his grandmother was taking her role of festival chairperson a little too seriously, but he now understood the reason for the gavel.

"What about a scavenger hunt?" Ethan suggested. "We could sell tickets. The proceeds could fund the jackpot."

"I like that." Chloe nodded. "Each business could sell tickets. Maybe have a special medallion created. The person who finds the medallion would win the jackpot."

"Sounds fun. A jackpot would attract more people. How much could we afford?" Rosie asked.

Elsie jotted down some notes. "I'll run some numbers and let you all know."

"I think writing clues would be something Paige would have fun doing," Chloe said.

"Perfect. Ethan, why don't you and Paige work together on the clues and where to hide them?" Elsie said.

"Sure, I can do that."

"Okay, what else?" Elsie glanced at her notes and looked to her grandson. "Has Abe thought of anything for the bookstore?"

"He hasn't mentioned anything to me. Paige might know."

Elsie looked to Chloe. "Chloe dear, don't you belong to a book group here at the bookstore?"

"I do." Chloe shifted in her chair.

Elsie asked, "What about an author signing?"

"That's a great idea," Emma and Rosie said in unison.

"Turner Books is the only small bookstore in the immediate area." Elsie glanced around the table. "Chloe, who was the author of the last book your group was reading?"

"We read a book by a new author, L.C. Brooks."

"Elsie, like my grandmother?" Ethan asked.

"No, L-C, the initials. She writes about small-town Minnesota. Abe can't keep her books on the shelf. Her third one is set to release on the first of July. I've already pre-ordered mine."

"Perfect timing," Elsie said.

"Um, I don't know how we'd get in touch with her," Chloe said.

Ethan noticed the silent communication between Chloe and the rest of the women at the table. He made a point of reading people. Interpreting signs was his life, and there was something going on between them he didn't understand.

Elsie waved dismissively. "Leave that up to Ethan and Paige. I'm sure they can talk this Brooks author into coming to sign books."

All the women around the table nodded.

"What kind of book is it?" Ethan asked.

"It's a sport romance. The first in the series is *Catch Me*, the second *Intercepted*," Chloe said.

Rosie picked up a piece of paper and fanned herself. "I read both, and they're wonderful. The hero is hot, hot, hot in all the best ways. He's also a baseball player." Rosie's brows bounced meaningfully as she looked Ethan's way.

As the ladies tittered over that, he ignored them and grabbed another glazed donut from the box.

"You know what? I can take care of getting in touch with the author," Chloe suggested.

"Don't be silly," Rosie said. "You have enough to do as a business owner yourself."

"Rosie's right. I'm sure Paige has contacts she can use if we have trouble reaching the author," Ethan said. "If the book is selling as well as you say, she may be the attraction we need to pull people in."

He might as well help out since he was the only one at the

table who didn't run a business. Paige had enough to deal with right now and if this author would attract people to the bookstore, he'd make sure she showed up, no matter what.

ABE INSISTED Paige drive him to the hospital in her grandma's 1968 Mustang. Paige didn't mind; she loved the fastback. Abe cracked the window open with a quick turn of the handle. She did the same. Paige didn't own a car in the city and missed driving the sleek black vintage vehicle along the country roads that curved around the lakes. The spring morning dew clung to the car, droplets running down the side windows.

Paige bit her bottom lip. She needed to confront her grandpa and wasn't sure how to bring up his finances, or lack thereof.

"You might as well spit it out," Abe said.

"Why do you always know when I have something to say?"

"Sweet pea, you always bite your bottom lip and crinkle your brow when you don't want to tell me something. Like when you fessed up to scratching the Mustang when you skimmed the mailbox. I wasn't mad then and I promise you I won't be mad now. You know you can tell me anything. So, what is it?"

They were twenty minutes into their forty-minute drive to the hospital. "I found the ledger on your desk." Paige took a deep breath. "Why would you send her money?"

"Waited until I couldn't escape, huh?" Abe said.

"I learned from the best."

"Here I thought you were going to tell me you're pregnant."

Paige rolled her eyes. "Oh, this tactic. I remember it well. You change the subject to something I will deny fervently or something I need to defend, and hope I'll forget what we were talking about." She chuckled. "I'm definitely not pregnant, and you need to answer the question."

"She's my daughter and she needed money."

"But—"

"But nothing. Someday you'll understand when you have children of your own." He seemed defeated, old, when he talked about her mother. She hated that Felicity caused him pain.

She and her grandpa never talked about her mother anymore. He respected Paige too much to mention Felicity. He and Paige's grandma had comforted her endless times when Felicity failed to show for her birthday parties and high-school graduation. Paige loved her grandparents for taking care of her when her mom decided she didn't want to be a mom anymore and left.

"There are some things you don't understand," Abe said.

"How about you help me to understand, then? I'm not a little girl anymore."

Paige worked hard and saved her money. She always had. She put herself through college by winning scholarships and working two jobs. Her mother, concerned only for herself, called infrequently and the conversations were always one-sided. Felicity was selfish and self-serving. Paige would only hear from her when she was between sugar daddies and needed money to maintain her lifestyle. When Paige started writing seriously, she decided to use a pen name so Felicity wouldn't find out, knowing that if she ever became a successful author, her mother would try to take advantage. Come to think of it, the last time Felicity had contacted her looking for a handout coincided with the dates in the ledger. After Paige refused to send money, Felicity must have gone to Abe.

"You know the bookstore has been handed down for generations," Abe said, interrupting her stewing.

She forced herself to loosen her grip on the steering wheel. "I do. I remember the stories you'd tell about my great-great-grandfather starting the bookstore shortly after the town was established."

"What you don't know is that the oldest has first dibs on the store. The store is passed from father to eldest son, or in my case, father to daughter. Legally, when I'm ready to retire, the store becomes Felicity's."

The oatmeal she'd had for breakfast threatened to reappear. "But . . . she hates it here, doesn't she?"

"She's made it abundantly clear she never wants to step foot in this town again."

Paige swallowed. "Okay, so what's the problem? I don't understand."

"She told me she wanted the store."

There it was again, the proverbial hand wrapped around her throat. "Why?"

"That's what I asked." He rubbed his leg.

Paige sighed. "She'd sell it and collect the money."

Her grandpa nodded. "I'm afraid so."

"Isn't there a way you can stop her?"

"I did. I met with our family lawyer and he advised me to sell the building. The original agreement didn't mention a building, only a store."

"So, you sold the building to Ethan."

"It was the only way I could pay your mother off. She got the fair market value of the store and signed away her rights. The bookstore is now yours if you want it."

"That's not going to stop her from asking for more." But it made sense and explained a lot. It explained why Ethan now held the deed to her family's legacy. If only her mother wasn't so selfish.

"No, I suppose it won't stop her, but I won't have any more to give and I made that very clear." Abe placed a hand on Paige's knee. "I understand if you don't want the bookstore. I know you have a home and career in New York."

Paige's stomach clenched. She didn't want to let her grandpa down, but she didn't know if she was ready to give up her life in New York. Financial security meant a lot to her, and she hadn't planned to leave her position at the publishing house yet. Margo had rejected her book, and while she had a strong readership and social media presence and her third book would be coming out soon, she couldn't afford to count on her writing or the bookstore for income. Just thinking about it stole her breath.

She took a moment to calm her nerves before answering, "It's not that I don't want Turner Books. You know I love the store—it was my safe haven and the place I got to spend time with you. I just don't know if I'm ready to take control."

"I'm hoping you at least consider it, but I don't want to pressure you into anything you don't want to do. The best thing I did was sell the building. Ethan has the means to get it back to its original glory," Abe said. "Heck, I suspect it will look better than it ever did."

They arrived at the hospital a few minutes later. Neither of them said another word about the bookstore and Paige was thankful. After her grandpa's appointment, she'd go for a run. Paige needed time to think before she met Chloe for trivia night.

CHAPTER FIVE

*P*aige slipped into a sleeveless emerald-green A-line dress. One of her favorites, she'd packed it on a whim and was glad she did. Wide halter straps skimmed over her and clung in all the right places. The vertical back straps held her snug and smooth in the front and accentuated her figure. She swished back and forth, admiring herself in her bedroom mirror. Her childhood room hadn't changed a bit. The woman she'd hired to clean the house every other week had also kept the dust in her room to a minimum and changed her sheets.

She reached for a hinged green-and-ivory flowered enamel bracelet from her grandmother's jewelry box and fastened it onto her wrist. A few of the costume jewelry pieces were a little too gaudy for her taste, but she'd take them to Chloe and allow her to work her magic. Paige couldn't wait to spend the evening with friends. She couldn't remember the last time she'd gone out on the town.

With time to spare, she applied a modest amount of makeup: a light foundation, mascara, and cappuccino lip gloss. She created a few wavy curls with a curling iron and headed downstairs. The smell of hamburger hotdish drifted through the house.

Her grandpa was sitting in his well-worn leather recliner reading the local newspaper, the *Lake Times*. "This town is going to hell in a handbasket."

"What makes you say that?" Jeez, she'd been gone too long. Why had she asked? She knew his propensity to talk a subject to death, and she didn't want to be late meeting Chloe. Maybe if she changed the subject she could escape.

"Developers are wanting to come in and buy up our lakeshore property," he said.

"Wouldn't that be good for the economy?"

"Our town was built on family businesses. The last thing I want is corporate developers stealing our property and destroying our landscape with cement and steel structures."

Saved by the oven buzzer, Paige asked, "Can I fix you a plate before I leave?"

"Smells wonderful, sweet pea. I'll make my way to the kitchen table."

Paige scooped a generous portion of hotdish onto a plate and buttered two slices of her grandpa's favorite sourdough bread, cut them in half, and set them on his plate. Abe always had buttered bread with his dinner. Her grandma used to set a plate stacked with slices of white bread in the center of the table beside her crystal butter dish at every meal.

Abe made his way to the kitchen, leaning the crutches on the table. Paige moved a chair with a cushion toward him and helped him prop up his leg.

She set the plate in front of him and sat down. "You look like you're getting around better."

"I think so. It was only a minor stress fracture. I'll be running around in no time." He placed the napkin on his lap, picked up his fork, and took a mouthful. "Thank you, it's very good. You look nice. Where are you off to tonight?"

"I'm meeting the girls for trivia night at the Eagle's Nest."

The cuckoo bird popped out of the kitchen clock, and Paige jumped. She hated that stupid bird. "I should probably get going. Can I set out anything else for you?"

"You're doing enough by taking care of the store. Go have fun and don't worry about me. Elsie said she'd stop over later."

After Paige's grandma Caroline passed away, Elsie and Abe's friendship had filled the void in their lives. They'd both been widowed for many years now, and Paige's romantic heart hoped there was something going on between the two. She loved Elsie like the substitute grandma she was, and it would be great to see them together.

On her way out the door, Paige grabbed her lightweight black sweater from the coatrack and placed it over her arm. Purse and keys in hand, she headed for town.

ON THE RIDE OVER, Paige must have seen at least a dozen people she recognized. She waved to Mr. Patton, her high-school math teacher, as he walked his bulldog down Fourth Street. Paige giggled; there was truth to the saying that dogs looked like their owners.

The Sampson brothers, who had to be in their nineties, were enjoying the mild spring night rocking on the porch swing of their home on Main Street. She'd always thought the old Victorian would make a wonderful bed-and-breakfast.

Everyone she passed waved. She'd forgotten the "Minnesota nice" wave of acknowledgement. It was a far cry from the hurried traffic of the city.

Paige parked her grandma's Mustang in front of Rural Chic Boutique and got out. Chloe must have seen her, because she stepped out of the store and locked the door. When the economy tanked a few years after Chloe returned from college, she bought the old building and lived in the apartment above. Then, a couple years back, Chloe opened her store.

"Look at you, girlfriend. You are rocking that dress," Chloe said.

Chloe always knew what to say. "Thanks. You look great too. I love your necklace. One of your designs?"

"Of course."

Chloe wore a mottled deep-turquoise V-neck tee layered over a dark purple tank, along with a waist-length black leather jacket, studded leather belt, black jeans, and black Converse high-tops. She made and sold her jewelry in her shop, and the leather-and-silver necklace she'd chosen rounded out her look.

The Eagle's Nest, located on the same block as the bookstore and down the street from Rural Chic Boutique, shared its interior walls with the buildings on each side of it. As they crossed the street, Paige breathed in the scent of greasy fries and burgers coming from the bar. "I didn't realize I missed the smell of grease." Her stomach growled.

"It's hard not to order takeout every night." Chloe said.

Chloe held the door open for Paige to enter.

The place was packed, with customers standing two-deep and chatting at the bar. The energy in the place was contagious. Paige's shoulders dropped away from her ears as she moved to the music.

Chloe held up two fingers to the bartender. "So *gor-geous*, don't you think? And single." Chloe fanned herself.

Paige snickered. "Yes, he's cute. But this place . . ." Her eyes darted around, taking in the space she remembered as being dark and dingy. "Wow. What happened? It's so light, and dare I say . . . chic?"

Chloe nodded. "It's great, isn't it?"

Maggie Reynolds and another woman waved to them from a length of high tables at the end of the glossy bar.

"Come on," Chloe said. "I'll introduce you to the remodeler. You might remember her from when she spent the summers here when we were teenagers." They made their way toward them. The din of the bar lessened as they approached the back corner of the room.

Maggie stood and hugged Paige.

"It's so nice to see you," Paige said.

"You too, Paige."

Maggie, the youngest of the Reynolds siblings and the only girl, stood a few inches taller than Paige and shared the same thick dark-brown hair and hazel eyes as Ethan. Maggie's long hair hung in perfect waves down her back.

Chloe introduced the other woman. "Paige. Do you remember Alexis Welby? She's the talented contractor who turned the Eagle's Nest into the hippest place in town."

Alexis shook hands with Paige. "My mom and I spent summers here in one of the Reynolds's cabins."

"Of course. It's nice to see you again."

The white lace-sleeved blouse Alexis wore didn't scream contractor, not that Paige had met a woman contractor before. But Alexis's ripped faded jeans and motorcycle booties completed her look of a beautiful badass. Paige admired her fun, tousled blonde bob with copper and caramel highlights. Paige scanned the room again. "This place is nothing like I remember it. You did an amazing job."

"Thank you."

Paige was about to take a seat when Ethan, Ethan's brother Zeke, and two of Chloe's brothers, Cole and Garrett Reid, sauntered through the front door.

It never failed; Ethan took Paige's breath away. She bit her bottom lip as she admired his sexy swagger. Paige pictured herself running her hands through his thick hair. His slick, muscled body against hers . . .

Chloe nudged her out of her fantasy. "Whatcha thinkin' about, Paige?"

Oh no, Ethan had caught her staring. He smiled, showing off his pearly whites. She was thankful for the subdued lighting, as he probably hadn't noticed her flushed cheeks.

"I need a drink."

"Oh, I know, it's the part in the book where his hands were all over you and—"

"Chloe!"

The guys stopped at the bar and ordered drinks. It was nice to see Ethan and Cole had stayed in touch, Paige thought as Cole slapped Ethan on the back and laughed. The Reids and the Reynolds boys were always good-looking, but as men, they were drop-dead gorgeous.

Cole, Zeke, and Garrett broke away from the group of women surrounding Ethan and joined them.

Cole and Chloe were close in age and because of the school cut-off in September, they ended up being in the same grade. Being best friends with Chloe, Paige had spent a lot of time with Cole too, especially when they were in grade school.

Cole swung an arm over her shoulder. "Paige, welcome back. It's nice to see you."

"Nice to see you too."

Cole's arm still draped over her shoulder, he turned to the rest of the table. "So, ladies, how about we make things interesting?"

"What do you have in mind?" Chloe said.

"How about guys against girls? The winners pick up the tab."

"Sure," Maggie said. "Are you expecting anyone else? We don't want to embarrass you."

Cole laughed. "Nope, four against four sounds about right, unless your boyfriend is coming. His name is Jared, right?"

"Yes, but he won't be joining us tonight. He's working late."

Ethan joined the group.

"Well, with Ethan on your team, you might be in trouble. I'm sure he'll be distracted, signing autographs all night," Paige said.

Ethan smiled. "You think so, Turner?" He lowered his voice and whispered, "You look nice."

His breath on her skin made her shiver. Before she could respond, a woman in a leopard-print blouse and cutoff jean shorts that barely covered her butt slid her way between them and thrust her chest toward Ethan. She handed him a pink Sharpie and pulled down her already low-cut shirt, revealing her ample breast until she was almost entirely exposed. "I would love it if you could sign here." She trailed a jewel-adorned, candy-apple red fingernail across her breast and giggled.

Ethan cleared his throat and signed his name.

"Thank you, hot stuff. Maybe I can keep you company tonight," the woman suggested.

Cole came to his rescue. "Trivia is about to start."

"Sorry, can't keep my friends waiting." Ethan dismissed the woman and took his seat.

Paige could feel her brow hit her hairline. If women acted this way around Ethan after retiring from baseball, no wonder he'd been branded as a ladies' man in the media. Ethan shifted nervously and created space between himself and the busty fan, whereas Allen would have enjoyed every second and might have taken the woman up on her offer. Ethan was one of the good guys, and Paige admired the way he handled the encounter, but that didn't mean she wouldn't razz him for his popularity. "Wow. Okay. Well girls, let's show these guys we're the smartest of them all."

Everyone raised their glasses. "Cheers! Let's get this game started!" Maggie said.

The music was lowered, and the waitresses handed out remotes as the TV screens around them flashed with the rules of the game. There were five categories: Entertainment, Science,

Sports, History, and Geography, with ten questions in each set. There would be bonus questions at the end to determine a tie, if needed. Team names popped up on-screen as the groups entered them into the computer. It looked like a good crowd had gathered to play.

Ethan entered his group name, "All-Stars." Maggie keyed in, "The Warriors," and Paige giggled. Maggie smiled and shrugged. "What? They're going down."

Chloe high-fived Maggie.

Alexis joked with Zeke.

Paige spotted Ethan looking at her. She raised her glass in a salute, and Ethan did the same.

The bartender spoke above the noise. "Let the games begin!" The first category was Entertainment, and the questions began to appear. Alexis proved to have the best knowledge of that subject. The guys had the least. After the first round, the Warriors were in second place and the All-Stars trailed behind in fourth.

A plate of nachos piled high with shredded chicken, cheese, jalapeños, tomatoes, and black beans was slid between the girls, along with plates and napkins. The waitresses amazed Paige by keeping up with the demanding patrons' drink and food orders.

Now that the first category was over, she looked forward to going against Ethan in Sports. No one had any idea how much she'd researched to write her three-book sports series. Chloe was the only one privy to her ongoing deception, but was sworn to secrecy.

The first sports trivia question flashed on the screen.

Against what opposing team did Babe Ruth hit his first career home run?

Zeke slapped Ethan on the back. "We got this!"

Paige quickly chose the New York Yankees and waited for the computer to show who answered the quickest.

Gasps were heard across the room when "The Warriors"

displayed on-screen. The girls cheered. Chloe high-fived Paige. "Yes!"

The next question appeared.

Who was the first Major League player to have his number retired?

The Warriors were first on the board again, taking the lead. Lou Gehrig's No. 4 was the first number retired on July 4, 1939.

Again and again, the Warriors nailed the answers, taking eight of the ten sports questions. Paige could feel Ethan's eyes on her. No way would she miss the next question while he gawked. Her girlfriends cheered. Chloe spouted sports metaphors like it was game day.

"Turner, how the heck do you know so much about baseball?" Zeke asked her.

Chloe sipped from her margarita and looked innocently at Paige. "Yeah Paige, how do you know so much about baseball?"

Paige kicked her friend under the table while everyone waited for an answer. "The last book I edited was a sports history book."

Ethan shook his head in disbelief. "You're making me look bad, Turner."

Paige took a drink of her vodka lemonade and eyed him over the rim of her glass. She was glad the sports questions were over. With all eyes on her, she wanted to bolt. Being the center of attention was never her idea of fun.

The last category was Art History. Maggie being a designer, Paige figured she would conquer the category, and she did. Maggie kept them in the lead, and they won the game.

Paige didn't know the last time she'd had this much fun with friends. She'd connected with Allen through work but beyond that, the demands of her job didn't lend themselves to close relationships; instead she spent her time reading and editing new fiction. Growing up, she'd had Chloe to make sure she left the confines of her house and the bookstore. Her "Chloe" in New

York ended up being charismatic Henry, who expounded that all work and no fun made Paige a dull girl. The rest of her co-workers thought her boring, and they no longer asked her to join them after work. Paige knew it was her fault for turning down the offers of after-work drinks, and she wished she hadn't been so focused.

Ethan called the waitress over and ordered a round of drinks and more appetizers for the group.

Chloe slid off her chair and whispered, "Hey, can I talk to you in private before I leave?" She gestured to the back hallway.

"Sure." Paige stood and followed her to the ladies' room.

Chloe pushed the door open and Paige followed her in. "I need to tell you something and I don't want you to freak out."

Chloe pushed on each stall door to make sure they were alone, and that worried Paige. "Okay, what's up? You're making me nervous."

"The committee wants L.C. Brooks as the guest author at the Fourth of July Festival."

"What?"

Chloe waved her arms and paced back and forth. "It wasn't my fault. Elsie asked me what the book club was reading, so I told them about *Catch Me*, and the whole thing spiraled out of control. I didn't know what to say. Then Ethan volunteered to contact the author. I said I would do it, but he said no, I had too much to do and he wouldn't mind. What was I supposed to say?"

"Slow down. Take a breath. Who exactly knows I'm the author?"

"Just me," Chloe said.

"Okay, it's okay." Paige started to pace. "How is Ethan going to contact me?"

"By email if he can, and if he can't reach L.C. Brooks, he's going to ask *you* if you know anyone who could help." Chloe bit her lower lip.

"Alright. I guess I wait for his email and then refuse to come because I'm too busy. That should work, right?" Paige fiddled with her bracelet.

"He was pretty determined to find you," Chloe said. "Oh yeah, I forgot, you and Ethan are working on the festival scavenger hunt, too."

Several women entered the restroom to reapply their lipstick, and Paige stood in the background, gaping like a guppy.

"Let's get back out there before they think we fell in," Chloe said.

"Good idea. I could use another drink," Paige croaked.

Two tall glasses of vodka lemonade with yellow sip straws waited for her at the table. Ethan strolled over. "Everyone keeps buying a round. I thought you had skipped out."

Paige picked up one of the glasses and removed the straw. She downed half the glass.

"You okay?" Ethan said.

"Yep, just thirsty." She pasted on a smile.

"What are your plans for tomorrow?"

"I have a lot to do at the bookstore. I plan on cleaning most of the day."

"Good. I had Alexis and Maggie draw up some renovation plans for the building and the bookstore. They'll be there by nine a.m., and I hope you can join us."

The thought of renovating the building worried Paige. She didn't see how the bookstore could stay open. As important as it was to her grandpa, she had to be realistic. Independent bookstores were closing everywhere.

How did everything get so out of control? She picked up the tall glass. Finding a way to save the bookstore, planning a scavenger hunt, keeping her identity secret, and finishing her third book in just over a month was proving too much. Her heart raced as she guzzled the drink in her hand.

"Sure. I'll be there." She finished her lemonade. She needed to leave. Paige stood and immediately grabbed the table to steady herself. Maybe she'd had too much to drink. She could probably stay at Chloe's . . . No. She needed to help her grandpa to bed. Crap.

"Come on, Paige. I'll take you home." Ethan removed Paige's sweater from the back of her chair and draped it over her shoulders, then slipped his arm around her waist.

She waved goodbye to everyone. "Thanks for the drinks! I had fun!"

Ethan gathered her close as he weaved them through the crowd.

"You smell good," Paige said.

SIX VODKA LEMONADES and an occasional appetizer was not a good combination. Not that Ethan was keeping track. Well, he was, but only because he couldn't keep his eyes off Paige. She had the attention of several men in the bar and had no idea. Ethan would sidle up to her when he saw an unfamiliar drunk approach, and slip his arm around her chair. No way would he let her out of his sight when she'd had too much to drink.

A cool breeze made Paige shiver as they stepped onto the sidewalk. Ethan tucked her into his warmth. The twinkle lights hanging from the ornamental trees gave off a soft, magical glow. Paige's blonde curls tickled his nose.

Paige pointed. "My car's that way."

Ethan steered her toward his truck. "How about you give me your keys and I'll bring your car by tomorrow."

"Okay."

Paige snuggled closer to him, her chin nuzzled his neck, and her breast grazed his chest. He pulled the passenger door open for her, and she reached for the top bar to pull herself up, but she slipped.

"Ohh, oops." She giggled as she fell back into his arms. "You caught me."

He stared into her brown eyes, liking the way her dark eyebrows complemented her golden locks. Her plush lips made him want to kiss her, but Ethan didn't take advantage of women who'd had too much to drink. He placed her on the seat and reached across her body to lock the seatbelt in place. He breathed in her sweet coconut scent.

By the time he had himself buckled in and the truck started, she was asleep, her head resting against the window. Ethan couldn't help himself; he reached over and tucked a stray curl behind her ear.

Abe had waited up for Paige. The lights of the television danced through the curtains of their living-room window. Paige snuggled against Ethan's chest as he carried her into the house.

"Who's there?" Abe asked from the living room. Well, the man wasn't hard of hearing. He probably recognized the Mustang hadn't been the vehicle that drove up.

"It's Ethan Reynolds, sir. Paige had a little too much to drink. I'll take her to her room."

"Thank you, son. That's not usually like her. Go on up, top of the stairs on your right."

If Ethan had his way, he'd be carrying her into his own house and straight to the bedroom. He had to keep reminding himself she didn't live in Deer Creek Falls and would be leaving soon. Maybe the chance to carry her over the threshold could happen— wait. Where the hell had that thought come from?

"Give me a few minutes, Abe, and I'll help you with anything you need."

"Thanks son, but I'm heading to bed now," Abe said.

"I'll lock up on my way out."

"Goodnight, Ethan. Thank you for looking after Paige tonight."

Ethan hadn't been in the upstairs of the Turner home before. He ran his hand along the wall for the light switch and hoped the light wouldn't wake Paige.

Wrapped up in baseball and the popular girls in high school, he now regretted that he hadn't seen Paige as more than a friend. A neighbor yes, but nothing more.

Her room sat above the front porch of the old farmhouse. The slanted ceiling and walls were painted a soft gray. Stuffed bookshelves lined two walls. Her bed was positioned in the middle of the room. He laid Paige on her bed, on top of the comforter, and pulled off her sandals. She didn't move. Her toenails were painted a hot pink. *Incredibly sexy*. Her dress had ridden up mid-thigh, showing more of her toned physique. He shifted uncomfortably and reached for the fluffy white blanket draped over the chair next to her dresser, pausing at a picture taped to her mirror. Chloe and Paige posed for the camera in their bathing suits on the end of the dock. He remembered that day well. It was Chloe's seventeenth birthday, and Paige walked down the boat ramp wearing a bright yellow bikini. The first time he noticed she had a figure. Cole had told him to turn away before he embarrassed himself.

Paige still had the same infectious smile. Tonight, her smile had lit up the room, and her laugh made him want her in a way he hadn't wanted anyone for a long time. When he left for Boston, she was still a wallflower, and now he couldn't keep his mind off her. The intelligent, funny, and beautiful woman in front of him had his body reacting.

He covered her with the blanket.

As he turned, he knocked a notebook off the bedside table. She didn't wake. He gathered the papers that had slipped from the notebook and noticed they were notes on characters of a story. Interested, he flipped through the pages and found a section named "Series Bible." Paige stirred and snuggled into her pillow. It was then he realized he was snooping. It looked as if she was writing. Good. He remembered the funny short stories she wrote for the school newspaper, and he'd always thought her name would look good on the bestseller list. He set the spiral notebook back on the nightstand and walked out of the room.

CHAPTER SIX

*P*aige woke in the middle of the night and changed into her pajamas. Bits and pieces of memory resurfaced. Ethan buckling her in, Ethan tucking her into bed. What had she done? What had she said to him?

She still reeled from the bomb Chloe had dropped the night before. Everything was spiraling out of control. She hadn't written a word since she'd arrived and the bookstore needed to be cleaned and organized, all while the building underwent renovations. She needed to run the store and sell enough books while her grandpa healed, or his efforts to save the business would be futile. She hoped what Ethan had planned didn't hinder sales.

Many tourists expected paperbacks to read while lounging on their boats or on the beach, and although they always sold a good number of them, it was hard to compete with e-book sales. But reading devices weren't ideal if the sun was shining, and there was always the threat of dropping them into the water. She'd had her share of close calls. Paperbacks would float at first when dropped in the water, easy to snag up, and they could still be dried. Cell phones or e-readers would sink like an anchor into the dark depths of the lake, unsalvageable.

Maybe she'd create some type of marketing campaign around paperbacks being the ideal mate on a boat. Hmmm . . . or maybe *mate* wasn't the right word when a swoon-worthy hunk like Ethan Reynolds sat beside you. Nobody could read with him in their line of sight.

More and more she began to warm to the idea of Ethan's plan to renovate the building. She couldn't figure out why he would want to buy it and sink a lot of money into fixing it up, but she would keep an open mind and see what Alexis and Maggie had planned for the space.

She dragged herself from bed and made her way downstairs to the kitchen. When she reached the bottom of the stairs, the smell of fresh-ground coffee wafted through the air.

"Good morning, sweet pea."

"Morning." Paige placed a kiss on her grandpa's cheek and beelined to the coffeepot. "Why are you up so early? Is your leg bothering you?"

"I'm always up this early. My leg is doing fine." His crutches leaned against the table, and his leg rested on a chair. "Late night?"

"Uh-huh." A cup sat next to the pot for her.

He could barely get around the small kitchen, yet he'd made coffee and set out a mug for her. Paige filled her cup and brought the pot to the kitchen table to top off her grandpa's. They sat at the antique oak table and stared into their mugs, watching the steam swirl and fade away. She'd missed mornings with Abe, when they discussed everything from politics to gossip heard at Rosie's the previous day, but a conversationalist she was not, this morning.

Abe broke the silence. "Didn't sleep well?"

"No."

"Want to talk about it?"

A whirlwind of thoughts hammered her. She didn't know how

to respond. What was she supposed to say? *Do you know L.C. Brooks? Well, she's me. I'm her. I didn't tell you because Ethan is the hero of my story. Oh, and hundreds of people have pre-ordered my third book and I'm having trouble coming up with an ending. And . . . if the bookstore is to survive it needs a facelift because it's run-down and isn't bringing in the people anymore, but then again independent bookstores everywhere aren't doing well, but how are we going to pay for new shelving and furniture?*

Paige put her head down on the table and let out a dramatic sigh. "Not really," she murmured.

Her grandpa patted her forearm. "Everything is going to work out, sweet pea, you'll see."

"I know. Thanks, Grandpa," Paige said.

"Ethan dropped the Mustang off this morning."

Paige sat up. "He did?"

Abe looked over the top of the newspaper and grinned. "Yep. Keys are on the table by the door."

She took another sip of her coffee. "That was nice of him."

Abe continued to read the paper. She got up and made him his usual: two eggs over easy, a slice of sourdough toast, and two slices of bacon. Thank goodness for frozen pre-cooked bacon. Zap it in the microwave for thirty seconds and voilà—perfection.

After breakfast, Paige followed him to his recliner to make sure he didn't fall. "Here's the TV remote and the new *Field and Stream* magazine."

"Thanks, sweet pea. Is today the day Alexis is bringing over the new plans?"

"Yep. Should I have her stop by later?"

"I trust you. Now get going and don't worry about me."

She scurried upstairs to get ready, dressing in a pair of jeans and a light-blue tee and pulling a light sweater and a watercolor floral scarf from her closet for when she opened the store.

"Alright, I'm leaving. Enjoy your game. Love you." She'd arranged for her grandpa's buddies to move their weekly card game from the café to the house so she didn't have to worry about him. She had enough to worry over.

THE LIGHTS WERE ALREADY on when Paige entered the bookstore. She set her bag down, hung up her sweater on the peg by the back door, and followed the music emanating from the front of the shop. Ethan held an invisible mic and belted out the words to "Start Me Up" by the Rolling Stones while he swayed his perfect tush to the music. She stood and watched. Very nice. Very nice indeed. When the song ended, Paige clapped.

Ethan turned. "Oh. Hi. I didn't hear you come in." He reached over and silenced his phone.

"I gathered." Paige grinned at his blush. She'd never seen Ethan blush before. Charming.

He reached around her and handed her a to-go cup of coffee that he had set on the front counter.

"Thank you. I never turn down coffee." She toyed with the hem of her T-shirt. "Thanks for driving me home. I guess I let loose last night. I've been a little stressed."

"Not a problem. You were cute."

Startled, she sputtered, "Cute? I'm embarrassed someone needed to take care of me. It's not something I'm used to." Paige took a sip. "This is great. Where did you get it?"

"I'm kind of a coffee snob, so I brought it from home."

"Bless you." Paige held the cup in both hands and breathed in the aroma. "How can there not be a coffee shop in town? And no bakery? What happened to Patty Cakes?"

"Patty moved to Florida to be closer to her grandkids." Ethan held up a white bag. "Rosie still makes her legendary cinnamon rolls, though."

"Oooh, gimme!" She grabbed the bag, opened it, and fished out a Styrofoam container. It might have been a little caveman of her, but she couldn't remember the last time she'd had one of Rosie's cinnamon rolls.

A lazy smile spread across Ethan's face. "It's all yours."

Paige leaped up, sat on the counter, and crossed her blue-jean clad legs. She had devoured half of the sugary and cinnamony goodness when Missy Covington sauntered through the door. One minute Paige was sighing with pleasure and the next, she found it hard to swallow. Missy Covington—head cheerleader, major head case, and the classic mean girl—made Paige's high-school years miserable. Missy sashayed over to Ethan.

"Oh Ethan! I was hoping to run into you!"

Ethan moved closer to Paige. "What can I do for you?"

"I heard you bought the building." Missy took in her surroundings. She wrinkled her nose and lowered her brows. "Oh, Paige, I didn't see you there. I see you're still shoveling it in."

Leave it to Missy to remember the extra pounds Paige carried in grade school. Sure, she'd been on the chubby side, but she had slimmed out in high school. She ran daily in order to eat the sugary treats she indulged in. Which reminded her, she needed to get a run in after she finished here today.

With her fingertips, Paige wiped the corner of her mouth.

Ethan turned and trailed his thumb over Paige's lip, removing the remaining frosting. "I got it."

She couldn't believe it when he licked the frosting from his thumb.

"Mmmm. Thanks for saving me some." He winked. Missy's mouth hung open, then closed.

Paige's whole body tingled from head to toe. She forgot they had an audience until the head case spoke again.

"Whatever. I see you came crawling home, Paige. Couldn't make it in New York City? Weren't you voted most likely to become a famous author? I guess it didn't pan out, huh?"

Missy swiped at her platinum-blonde hair, styled to perfection. She glanced at the mess of boxes. "I don't think you can save this place. It's horrid." She wiggled her three-carat diamond ring in front of Paige's face. "Did you hear I'm engaged to Ronnie Baker? He owns the only car dealership in town."

It took everything for Paige to smile. "Congratulations. You're perfect for each other." Paige felt sick to her stomach.

"What did you need, Missy? We need to get back to work," Ethan said.

"Oh, yes of course. There is a lot of work to do, isn't there? I was hoping you'd have the second book by L.C. Brooks, *Interception*. I get goose bumps when I read the scenes between the hero and heroine." She placed a hand on Ethan's forearm. "I pictured you while reading the first book." She sighed. "Have you read her books, Paige?"

Paige's stomach churned. "I have. Several times in fact. I'm pretty sure I've memorized them by now." She noticed Ethan watching her.

"I bet you wish you could write that good!"

"Yep, I sure wish I could write that *well*. Let me get that book for you." Paige jumped off the counter, grabbed the book from the display, and quickly rang it up.

"I have some paperwork to do. Excuse me." As Paige walked away, she heard Ethan tell Missy he was planning to contact L.C. Brooks and ask her to do a signing of her third release at Turner Books. Missy screamed with delight. Paige headed for the bathroom as the cinnamon roll threatened to make a reappearance.

As Paige made her way back to the front of the store a short while later, she heard the bell jingle. Alexis came through the door with the plans held high. "Good morning!"

Paige thanked her lucky stars when she saw Alexis and Maggie walk in. She didn't need another blast from the past. "Good morning. You sound entirely too chipper after last night's festivities." Paige removed a stack of books from the front counter to make room for Alexis to spread out the plans.

"We've already downed a pot of coffee at Rosie's. She made us the ultimate hangover breakfast—avocado toast and a side of fruit."

"I probably should have had that instead of the cinnamon roll," Paige said.

"Don't let her fool you. She was moaning earlier." Ethan smirked.

Alexis and Maggie looked between the two of them.

"Over the cinnamon roll," Ethan clarified.

"How do you always end up with the last of the cinnamon rolls?" Maggie asked her brother.

Ethan laughed. "I'm Rosie's favorite."

Maggie stuck her tongue out at Ethan as Alexis unrolled the plans then anchored them with a nearby stapler and a few paperbacks.

"I'm excited to see your ideas," Ethan said.

"Great. I think you'll like them," Alexis said. "Should we get started?"

"Absolutely," Paige and Ethan said at the same time.

Alexis stepped to the edge of the carpet and pulled on a loose corner. "We'll start by pulling up the carpet to reveal these original hardwood floors beneath." She motioned to the walls. "I'd like to keep some of the exposed brick as accents but cover a portion with drywall."

"And paint the walls a light aqua," Maggie said. "We'll whitewash the exposed brick to lighten the space and offset the coffee-brown finish of the hardwood."

Alexis continued, "We'll open the ceiling, expose the rafters, and paint the ductwork black. Black track lighting will shine onto the built-in bookshelves. Pendant lighting will hang from the ceiling by black cords."

"The lights will give the feeling of a starry sky," Maggie said.

They all looked at the water-stained ceiling tiles.

"Will the roof need to be replaced?" Paige asked.

"Yes. I included it in the bid. Abe couldn't remember when it was replaced last."

Alexis handed a copy of the bid to Ethan, who tucked it into his back pocket. "The rest will be cosmetic, and that's Maggie's area of expertise," she said.

"I've asked Cole to make heavy-looking butcher-block tables on casters," Maggie said. "Scattered around the bookstore will be comfy wingback chairs. Strips of chalkboards will run between the top shelf cubbies and the bookcases. It'll be a mix of old and new." She smiled.

"Oh, when we were measuring the back rooms, I noticed a collage of photos. Your grandpa is pictured with several famous authors. I would love to incorporate those photos on a wall near the front of the store so everyone could appreciate them. Do you think it would be okay with Abe?"

"I think he would love that. I always thought they should be displayed for everyone to see."

Paige loved the vision they provided for the bookstore, but wondered if she hadn't returned home, would she have known Ethan had bought the building and hired a renovator and designer? She had ideas. What about her vision? Ethan owned the building, not the bookstore.

Ethan bumped shoulders with her. "Hey, you okay?"

"Yep. I'm fine."

Maggie glanced at Alexis, then at Paige. "We get pretty excited and tend to take over, but by all means, these plans aren't set in stone. Abe asked us to work up something, but please know he asked that you have final say. He expects you to sign off on everything to do with the design."

Paige realized she was being petty. Besides, she shouldn't care; she had a job and life to return to in New York. "I've loved everything you've presented. Please, continue."

Alexis pointed to the drawing she'd unrolled earlier. "Right here will be the kids' corner."

Ethan nodded. "I like that. Maybe we can get input on the design of this area from Nikki and Nora. I'd also like to make sure there are plenty of cozy nooks to read in like there were when we were growing up."

"That's a great idea," Maggie said.

Paige was touched he'd remembered that about the store, and she liked that he'd thought to include his ten-year-old twin nieces in the decision-making process.

Alexis motioned to the large window Abe used to display the bestsellers. "The front window needs replacing. I'd like to add a window film to dramatically reduce the sun's rays and protect the window displays, furniture, and hardwood floors from fading."

"You won't be able to tell there is film on the windows, and it's manufactured here in Minnesota," Maggie said.

"Good. I like the idea of keeping most of the project local," Paige said.

Alexis nodded. "My subcontractors live in Deer Creek Falls or in surrounding communities, and of course Zeke will be the electrician. I buy my materials from local businesses when I can."

"Alexis and I rescued some great chandeliers from an old home in Duluth. With a little TLC they'll be perfect for this space." Maggie motioned to the area above where they stood. "We'll place one over the front counter."

"This sounds like it will take a long time and a lot of money," Paige said.

"I'm taking care of the remodel," Ethan said.

"That's ridiculous. You own the building, not the store." Paige truly liked the vision they painted, but knew from her grandpa's ledgers he didn't have nearly enough to cover such a facelift.

"How long are we talking, Alexis?" Ethan said.

"We're shooting for six to eight weeks, and that's putting my entire crew on the job. The heating system needs to be replaced and we'll want to add central air. The electric and plumbing also need replacing. Basically, the entire building needs to be overhauled."

"Do you think we should start the remodel during our busiest season?" Paige asked. "The tourists make this our best time of year for paperback sales."

Ethan nodded. "You're right, and that's why I leased the space next door. It's perfect because it used to be a souvenir shop; the owner left tables and shelves. It'll work to put enough books on the shelves to draw people's attention, and it has a small window for display."

He'd thought of everything.

They said their goodbyes to Alexis and Maggie. Paige took a few calming breaths and tried to think of how to phrase what she needed to say to Ethan without sounding ungrateful.

She turned to him. "Abe told me why he had to sell the building and I appreciate you buying it and remodeling it, but we don't have the money to transform the inside the way Alexis and Maggie described."

"Hey." Ethan hooked his finger under her chin and lifted her gaze. At his touch, her body warmed all the way to her toes, stopping at every important detour along the way. Flecks of green and gold danced in his hazel eyes. She could lose herself in those eyes. "Abe warned me already, but you're not the only one with fond memories of this place. I *want* to do this. Please allow me to do this for Abe."

Paige bit her lip. "How can I help?" She leaned inward.

The sound of the front door made them jump apart. "Hello Ms. Johnston, what can we help you find this morning?" Ethan said.

"I came to see if the book I ordered has arrived. Paige dear, how are you? The Town Talk app said you were back in town. To stay, I hope?"

"I believe I saw a book set aside with your name on it in the back. I'll go check," Ethan said.

Ms. Johnston had been Paige's fourth-grade teacher and the one who inspired her to write. The requisite glasses still hung from a chain around her neck.

"I'll be here another month to help Abe, but then it's back to work, I'm afraid."

Ethan joined them again with book in hand and removed the Post-it note that read "paid," written in Abe's scrawl. "Here you are."

"Thank you, dear, and thank you again for replacing those rotted porch boards."

"No problem, Ms. Johnston. I'm available to help when you need me. I enjoy your chocolate chip cookies, too." Ethan patted his stomach.

"You're a good boy." Ms. Johnston pinched his cheek like he was twelve, turned, and hobbled out of the store.

"Ethan Reynolds, you're a good boy." Paige smiled.

"I'm good at a lot of things." Ethan waggled his brows.

It was her turn to blush. Oh boy, she needed water before she spontaneously combusted.

Ms. Johnston had rotten timing. Ethan had wanted to kiss Paige. He knew she'd be returning to New York and he'd told himself to ignore his attraction, but he found it impossible in the little time he'd spent with her, and they hadn't even begun working on the scavenger hunt yet.

He hoped she was single and that the absence of a ring on her finger wasn't because her boyfriend couldn't commit. She hadn't mentioned a boyfriend at the Eagle's Nest last night.

"Where do you want to start?" Ethan pulled a book from a shelf and blew dust from its cover.

"Well, that isn't very popular, is it?" She laughed. "Let's get several boxes started, books that we'll move next door, sell online, or donate to the library in Willow Creek."

"Sounds good. I'll grab some boxes."

They talked as they pulled books from shelves and sorted them.

"It's funny Missy mentioned L.C. Brooks," Ethan said. "That's the author Chloe talked about at the committee meeting. I wondered if we could get her in as a guest author during the festival. All the ladies at the meeting seem to like her books. It may be what we need to bring people in." Maybe he was being too aggressive using the word "we," but he owned the building, and "we" sounded right.

"Yes, she mentioned something last night."

"Do you know the author?" Ethan taped a box shut and stacked it against the wall. "Paige?"

"Hmmm?"

"I wondered if you knew the author. The only contact information she has is an email address. I thought I'd email her later."

"Oh. She's . . . not a Cagney and Cahill author."

They worked in tandem for hours, making small talk as they packed boxes. A few customers wandered in to browse, but they still were able to make a large dent in their sorting and packing efforts, clearing most of the bookcases. The current titles remained at the front of the store on a few tables and paperback racks.

They moved to the children's section.

Ethan handed her *The Hungry Caterpillar* and Paige's stomach growled. She giggled.

"I'm hungry too," he said. "How about I call Mario's? He makes the best pizza around."

"That good, huh?"

"I think you'll be surprised. Mario definitely hits it out of the park."

"Oooh . . . now you're playing hardball." Paige smiled. "Better than a New York pie?"

"Just as good. Don't worry, he won't drop the ball."

"I don't know, Reynolds; New York pies are in a league of their own."

"What kind of toppings do you like?"

"Surprise me. I'm not picky."

Who would have thought he'd have so much fun packing up a bookstore?

Paige stood on a stool to retrieve a book from the top shelf. With his hand on the small of her back to steady her, he reached for the book. "Here, I got it. We don't need any more accidents."

Ethan noticed her curves and the way her shirt rode up, exposing her belly button. He wanted to run his hands along her smooth skin and trail them further north.

Paige stepped down and stretched. They'd been working nonstop since before noon. He surveyed the area; they'd put quite a dent in the old shop. He'd caught her watching him as he hauled boxes to the back room. What would she do if he pulled her close and kissed her? He was afraid he wouldn't want to stop. Until the evening of the senior party he hadn't given Paige much thought. Something primal had coursed through him that night. The urge to protect her. He was so confused he didn't know what to do, but it was too late. He left town the next day to play baseball, and they'd never talked about it since.

MARIO ARRIVED WITH THEIR PIZZA. Dressed in black, Mario resembled a younger De Niro with his large nose and quizzical look. Paige wanted to blurt out, "I'm a fan!" but she controlled herself.

Mario handed the pizza to Ethan and took Paige's hand in his. "Abe has shown me many pictures. You are even more beautiful in person. Ethan's a lucky man." Mario bowed and placed a kiss on Paige's hand.

"Oh, we're not—"

Ethan interrupted, "Thanks, Mario."

The aroma of spicy pepperoni and onions filled the bookstore, covering the dust-and-mildew smell. So much better. Her stomach growled as Mario snapped a white linen tablecloth onto the table they had cleared. He pulled out two battery-operated taper candles from his back pocket and rummaged around his bag. Mario uncorked a bottle of red and placed it on the table with two wine glasses.

Mario placed a hand over his chest, "Ahh. Young love. Enjoy your date." He winked. "Ciao!"

Paige blushed at the thought that Ethan had planned this. When she wrote the book and modeled her hero after her high-school crush, she never imagined sitting across from him in the bookstore's cozy reading nook, sharing pizza by *candlelight*. She could ignore the little tingle of pleasure, or roll with it and enjoy the moment like her heroine would. Ethan was hero material, all right.

Paige picked up the slice of pizza Ethan placed on her plate. She chewed her first bite and savored the taste of the mozzarella, spicy pepperoni, sweet peppers, onions, and salty olives. She groaned. "Mmmm . . . this is delicious." She dabbed at her mouth with her napkin.

The corner of Ethan's mouth tilted. "Told you." Ethan took a bite of his pizza. "Mario does good business even in the winter months when there aren't as many tourists."

"I can see why. He really pulls out all the stops."

Ethan smiled. "So tell me, Paige, what does your job entail? I know you're an editor. But what do you edit and what's involved?"

Paige set her pizza down and took a sip of her wine. She kept her glass near her lips as she studied Ethan. "I edit fiction. Mainly thrillers."

"I bet that keeps you up at night."

"You're not kidding. I've learned to save the scary passages until I get home and am tucked safely into bed."

Ethan finished his glass of wine and set it down. "I can only imagine." He leaned back in his chair and looked into her eyes. "Do you read anything lighter to counteract the terror?"

Paige leaned forward and blushed. "I do. I read romance to help me relax."

"Have you done much writing yourself? I heard most voracious readers tend to try their hand at it."

Paige cleared her throat. "I have a few stories in the works." She waved him off. "Enough about me—tell me what it's like to make all your dreams come true."

She focused on Ethan's mannerisms as he went into tales of his teammates and locker-room antics. He confided how much he missed his family during the season, and how nice it was to play in a city where at least one of his brothers resided. She was mesmerized by his voice and his deep, genuine laughter as he caught her up on all the Reynolds brothers. Roman, who ran the family landscape business; Isaiah, a doctor in the Twin Cities; and Luke, who Ethan spent the most time with when living on the East Coast. He shared stories of when Zeke and Maggie visited him in Boston, and how he'd threatened his single teammates with bodily harm if they asked his sister out.

Lightning flashed in the distance. Paige counted a few rumbles of thunder, five seconds. "It's getting closer."

Ethan filled their glasses. "I love the rain."

"Me too."

He placed another slice on her plate. "I'd forgotten you were voted most likely to become an author until Missy mentioned it earlier."

She needed to tread lightly. Paige wouldn't lie to Ethan, but she wasn't ready to tell the whole truth, either. "Yep, with the name Paige Turner and spending most of my free time here"—she gestured to the bookshelves—"I was destined for the label."

"And the fact that your face was constantly buried in a story," Ethan said.

Paige laughed. "That too."

Paige's phone beeped. She turned it over and glanced at the text message.

"Do you need to respond?"

"No. It's Henry. I'll call him when I get home."

Ethan nodded, and his gaze drifted over the room before returning to hers. "Is Henry your boyfriend?"

"No, a friend and colleague."

Was Ethan jealous? She never thought she could make Ethan Reynolds jealous. Paige was the green-eyed one in high school when he hadn't noticed her. Or never noticed her as girlfriend material, anyway. In later years when she stalked him on social media, he always had a blonde on his arm.

"So, no boyfriend?" Ethan leaned closer, took her hand in his, and traced circles on her palm.

Flustered, she answered, "Nope, no boyfriend. Not anymore."

"Bad breakup?"

"You could say that, but at least nobody was privy to it. I'm sorry your breakup was splashed across the tabloids."

"It is what it is. I'm happy I'm away from the gossip rags and that we've established we're both single, because I've been wanting to kiss you all day." He leaned over the table, gazed into her eyes, and awaited her permission.

Her heart raced as she leaned in and their lips met. Never in her life had she experienced the electricity she felt when his lips brushed hers. He deepened the kiss and their tongues clashed for dominance. With the yearning that had been building inside her all day, she wanted to leap across the table and devour him.

A loud crash made them jump apart, and the lights flickered then went out. Tiles fell from the ceiling and crashed to the floor.

A slow but steady stream of water landed on Ethan's head and trickled down his shirt. He leapt from his chair.

Paige cupped her hand to her mouth, doing a half-assed job of hiding her surprise and laughter. Flushed from the toe-tingling kiss, she handed Ethan a napkin.

Ethan accepted the soggy napkin and burst out laughing. "Talk about making an impact. That was one unforgettable kiss."

They used the flashlights on their phones as they gathered buckets and garbage cans and placed them under the areas where water trickled.

Paige would glance his way and he'd wink as they worked in tandem, cleaning the mess. The ongoing thought of sharing another kiss with Ethan made her cheeks stain a light pink.

"The roof has just moved to the top of the list," Ethan said.

"I think that's a brilliant idea."

CHAPTER SEVEN

A parade of sexy men entered the old souvenir shop to help move inventory from Turner Books to the new space. Ready to start renovation, Alexis needed the store cleaned out, and on this warm spring day when they could have been fishing and spending time relaxing, their friends were helping. Paige was humbled by their generosity and had to wipe away a tear that managed to escape.

Maggie and Paige unpacked books for the window display. Maggie fanned herself as she watched Cole and Garrett walk by. Their ripped biceps bulged under their tight T-shirts.

"I have to admit, the men in this town are worthy of more attention than any man in New York," Paige commented.

"I don't know, there are plenty of sexy rich men in Manhattan," Maggie said.

"Still, there's something about men who do physical work that does it for me," Paige said.

"Yeah, all those kegs Garrett lifts at his brewery. I can't believe someone hasn't snatched him up yet," Maggie said, her gaze fixed on Garrett's muscles.

"Whoo-hoo," Elsie called out as she entered the store clutching a large box. "Can someone help me with this?" Garrett rushed over to take the box from her. "Thank you, sweetheart."

Elsie winked at Paige. The woman must have ESP—either that or they were being way too obvious ogling the men. "Try dropping something, dear. I'm sure Ethan will come to your rescue," she whispered.

Paige rolled her eyes and looked to Maggie. "It's not a terrible idea." Maggie chuckled.

Elsie unrolled a poster. "Paige dear, hand me the tape from my bag. I need to hang this on the window."

Paige retrieved the tape dispenser. "What is it?" she asked then stopped short, taking it in.

The poster showed the silhouette of a woman with a question mark in place of her face and large, bold letters underneath that said, "USA Today Bestselling Author L.C. Brooks Coming Friday, July 3."

"I have high hopes Ethan will convince the author of *Catch Me* to come to our festival," Elsie said.

Paige fumbled with the tape dispenser; it fell to the floor.

Elsie smiled mischievously. "Paige dear, you need to drop something heavier than that to get the men's attention."

"Think what a draw this author would be," she continued. "Abe can't keep her books on the shelf. It's like when Danielle Steel had a new book out and the tourists would swarm like a flock of seagulls into the store. Remember that?"

Ethan came by and set a large box on the front counter. It flattered Paige that Elsie would compare her to Danielle Steel. But it didn't help the panic rising to the surface. Chloe had filled her in on Ethan's mission to find the author, but she hadn't thought posters would already be made. Paige had intended to reject the invitation as soon as Ethan emailed L.C. Brooks. She still would. She would pay to have posters remade for another author.

Paige jumped when Ethan said, "It's my job to track this author down, but so far, I've had little luck. I've emailed her but haven't gotten a response. Paige, maybe you could help me figure out a way to talk an author into revealing herself and coming to our sleepy little town."

Geez. She'd forgotten to check her author email. She needed to reply with a resounding no to Ethan's invite and put all this nonsense behind her. She felt bad that Elsie had spent money on the faceless author posters, but she couldn't come forward. Not now with things developing with Ethan. It was no secret that he'd been deceived by his ex-fiancée; she could only imagine how he felt about that. Besides, if the town knew she wrote *Catch Me*, they would figure out she based her hero on him.

"That's a wonderful idea." Elsie looked from Ethan to Paige. "Paige, you must have some contacts who could help."

"Um, sure. But maybe she doesn't want people to know who she is. I've encountered several authors who like to remain anonymous."

"If you wrote a book, would you want to remain anonymous?" Ethan asked Paige.

"There are several reasons authors choose to hide their identities." Paige opened the box of new releases Ethan had set next to the front display table and began stacking the books, hoping the conversation would end.

The screwdriver Maggie was using to put the wire paperback rack together slipped. "Ouch." Maggie shook her hand. "Ethan, did you find an author website? A social media presence?" Maggie asked.

Ethan handed Paige a stack of books. "Yeah, and I used the email address listed on her contact page, but I haven't heard back."

Elsie stood back to admire the poster and waved to a passerby. "Hmmm, does it say where she lives? Her likes and dislikes? Her favorite things? Maybe we can narrow it down. Find another way to connect with her."

Great, Elsie was going to go all Nancy Drew on the case of the mystery author. The sweet woman could be relentless about getting her way. Paige was now in full panic mode as she thought back to what her author page revealed.

"What do you think, Paige?" Elsie asked.

Ethan shrugged and said, "Who knows, maybe she's on vacation and hasn't checked her fan mail." He smirked as if he knew something, but he couldn't know, could he?

"Ethan's right, maybe she hasn't had time to check her email." Paige excused herself and found a quiet corner in the back of the building. She opened L.C. Brooks's email. There were three messages from a Fenway11. Fenway Park and Ethan's jersey number. Yep, from Ethan. She opened the email:

DEAR L.C. BROOKS,

Hello, Ms. Brooks. My name is Ethan Reynolds and I work closely with our Minnesota town's independent bookstore, Turner Books. I understand the third book in your sports romance series is set to release on July first. Our customers love your books, and here at Turner Books, we can't keep them on the shelf! Since your upcoming release coincides with our annual Fourth of July festival—one of the largest in the area—we would like to extend an invite to you to launch Power Play *here in Deer Creek Falls. We will purchase multiple copies of all three books in your series to have on hand for you to sign.*

Our town borders one of the largest lakes in MN, hosts over fifteen thousand people in the summer months, and we throw one of the biggest Fourth of July festivals in the area.

We'd like you to be a part of our festival by being our guest author, with your choice of accommodation: a beautiful lakeside

condominium at the Deer Creek Lodge or a peaceful, newly reno-
vated two-room cabin on Balsam Lake. Your airline ticket and
speaker fee will be covered.

We hope you will consider Deer Creek Falls as the destination
to launch your third book. Please feel free to email me with any
questions.

Thank you for your consideration. I look forward to hearing
from you soon.

Sincerely,
Ethan Reynolds on behalf of Turner Books

She opened the second email:

DEAR L.C. BROOKS,

I'm wondering if you received my first email. I'm hoping it
isn't in your junk mail folder and this doesn't end up there, too.
My job on the festival committee is to contact you and try to
arrange a book signing during our July fourth festivities. I read
your bio and it says you live in New York. I'm hoping I can
persuade you to visit our small lakeside town. Free airfare, free
lodging. If you'd like to stay a week, I can make that happen.
We're known for our extensive bike trails, fishing, hiking, and
waterskiing. I can arrange any or all of these activities for you.
Deer Creek Falls is a great place to relax and/or write your next
book. Please let me know soon.

Thanks,
Ethan

PAIGE GLANCED up to make sure nobody had come to find her and
opened the third email. He was definitely persistent.

. . .

Dear L.C. Brooks,

Sorry about all these emails, but I wanted to include the links to the accommodations I'm offering.

Looking forward to hearing from you,
Ethan

She typed a quick reply:

Dear Ethan,

Thank you for your generous offer. Deer Creek Falls sounds wonderful and the lodge looks breathtaking. I really wish I had the time. I was planning to launch my third book without any fanfare. I have family commitments that require my full attention. I would be happy to give you a list of authors who may be available for your Fourth of July Festival. Please let me know if I can help in another way. Thank you for thinking of me. I truly am flattered.

Regards,
L.C. Brooks

PAIGE HURRIED BACK out front so she wouldn't be missed. Chloe wasn't around to run interference.

A steady stream of women filed through the store. Paige guessed the men were the main attraction. At least the customers were purchasing books. Whatever it took. Maybe she needed to hire hot guys to stock shelves more often.

Throughout the day, she enjoyed engaging with the customers when they asked her questions about the author they were promoting. She'd missed talking about books and interacting with patrons.

Editing in a cubicle and conversing with Henry or chatting

with Charlie over coffee were the only interactions she encountered most days in New York, since Allen had traveled a lot. Occasionally, she'd strike up a conversation at the market. Even then she received one-word answers from the people there, unlike the townspeople she grew up with.

ETHAN WIPED his hands on his jeans while noting the time. The sun cast long shadows down the sidewalk out front, and the team looked well-worn from an honest day's work. They had made decent progress while keeping the bookstore up and running.

"Ethan," Garrett called. "This is the last box from next door. How about calling it a day?"

"Yeah, sounds good, man. Let's gather the team and see what they have in mind for dinner."

Zeke was standing close to Paige with his arm draped over her shoulder. "What do you say, Turner? Bonfire at the parents' house tonight?" Ethan noticed the playful exchange between his brother and Paige and didn't like it. Not one bit. *Time to break it up.*

Elsie interrupted. "That's a great idea, Zeke, but it's ladies' night at your mom's place. I'm making my way there next."

"How about if everyone comes to my place? It's the least I can do to say thanks for helping us out today," Ethan said.

"Sounds great." Paige turned her attention away from Zeke and asked, "What time do you want us there?"

"Let's clean up and meet in an hour." Damn. He should have told her to come earlier so they'd have some alone time.

"I'll text Alexis," Maggie said. "This will be so much fun!"

Paige reached for her phone. "I'll let Chloe know."

Elsie placed a hand on Ethan's arm. "I'll drop off your favorite dark-chocolate caramel brownies."

The night was looking better and better with the promise of

good food and friends. Ethan kissed his grandmother on her cheek. "You know I can't resist your brownies." He grinned.

CHAPTER EIGHT

*P*aige walked along the well-worn trail through the woods between the Turner and Reynolds places, carrying a covered salad bowl in one arm—her contribution to the spontaneous dinner party. She breathed in the new-growth smell of the pine trees, fingering the soft sprigs. Abe had told her Ethan had bought the property on the other side of the Reynolds cabins. She followed a cleared path along the lake. When she reached the cabins, the sun had started to retreat into the horizon. She knew she'd be late, but she couldn't help but stop and take in the tall evergreens lining the western shore of Balsam Bay. Paige missed the sunsets and sunrises over the lake. Would she miss skyscrapers if this were her view every day?

The loons called and the water lapped against the shore. The first of the cabin guests prepared their boats for the next day's fishing outing at the docks.

A cool breeze off the lake sent a shiver up her spine.

Maggie came around the corner from the smallest cabin and waved. "Hi, Paige! I was just heading over to Ethan's."

Paige waited for her to catch up. "No Jared tonight? I was hoping to meet him."

"He's working late and doesn't think he'll make it."

"That's too bad. Another time then." Paige shivered. "The bonfire will feel great. It's supposed to dip into the low fifties tonight." She gestured to the cabin Maggie had come from. "Are you living in Cabin Twelve?"

"I am! I've been renovating and decorating the cabins—under Alexis's supervision, of course," Maggie said. "I started with my grandpa's cabin and made it my own."

"Abe told me about your grandpa Reynolds. I was sorry to hear about his passing. He was such a nice man. He adored you."

Maggie smiled. "Thanks, Paige. Yes, I was his little girl."

She motioned to the carved wooden cabin sign. "What do you think about these? Cole made them for me."

"They're beautiful. I knew Cole was a woodworker but didn't realize he carved, too."

"He does. Wait until you see the bear he carved with a chainsaw. It's in Ethan's front yard."

Paige followed Maggie down a small deer trail through a grove of birch trees, which led to an open expanse carpeted in green. Ethan's property. Paige admired the grandeur of his house.

"It's amazing, isn't it? It takes my breath away every time," Maggie said.

"This isn't what I imagined. Wasn't this Old Man Carter's place? I remember a small log cabin with hand-hewn logs, not this." Massive boulders surrounded the foundation of the three-story log home, and windows spanning the height of all three levels reflected the red-and-orange sunset across the lake.

"Come on, wait until you see the interior. Ethan incorporated part of the old cabin into the new, keeping several of the original walls."

They waved to Chloe and Cole, who were tending to the bonfire by the lake, and headed inside.

MAGGIE AND PAIGE climbed the steps to the expansive deck, where Ethan and Zeke stood chatting, beers in hand. "Hey, beautiful." Zeke smiled.

Paige looked behind her and then back to Zeke. A pinkish tint spread up her neck. The look on her face . . . priceless.

Ethan didn't blame his brother. Paige's long, wavy blonde hair, brown eyes, and incredible figure, mixed with her intelligence and the way she genuinely cared for her friends and family, were intoxicating. Paige didn't realize how attractive she was, and he liked that a lot. He was used to women who flaunted their looks. They knew they were beautiful and used it to their advantage.

Maggie pulled a bottle of wine from the bag over her shoulder and handed it to Ethan. "Can you open this and grab two glasses?"

"Sure. Let's head into the kitchen."

He pulled a corkscrew from a drawer and opened the wine. "Paige, can I pour you a glass?" Ethan asked.

"It's a sweet red from a local winery. It's one of my favorites," Maggie said.

"I would love a glass, thanks. Sorry I'm late. I got caught up in emails from my editor and had to take care of a few things."

"No need to apologize, it was a casual start time. Can I take that?" Ethan gestured to the bowl in her hands.

"Oh, yes. Thanks. It's just a pasta salad I whipped up."

"Perfect. I'll put it in the fridge until we're ready to eat."

Zeke asked, "You mentioned an editor? Do you write?"

"Did you write a book, Paige? How exciting," Maggie said.

Paige flushed. "Oh. I'm referring to my boss. She's an acquisitions editor. I'm wrapping up a few things for work."

Zeke popped a cube of cheese into his mouth from the charcuterie board on the island. "What kind of books do you edit?"

"Mainly thrillers."

"I love thrillers. Any books I may have read?"

"Have you read the Saperstein series?"

"Great books, I've read them all. I can't believe you get to read them first. I'm jealous."

Ethan loved how animated Paige became when she talked about books. He could tell she enjoyed her job and knew it was only a matter of time before she would return to New York. Dating his ex, Bridgit, when he was on the road had resembled a long-distance relationship, and look how that turned out. Could he make one work with Paige?

"I wish you would write," Maggie said with a laugh. "I still remember the stories you'd tell when you babysat me. You always had a great princess story, and I'd fall asleep dreaming of castles and fairies. I used to think you wrote *Cinderella*!"

Paige chuckled. "I wish."

Zeke moved closer to Paige.

Ethan looked at his brother. "Zeke, why don't you gather everyone from outside, and I'll start the grill." He handed Maggie and Paige their wine.

"I can do that. Paige, do you want to walk with me to the beach?" Zeke said.

Maggie spoke up. "Why don't you go ahead, Zeke? I want to show off my design skills and give Paige a tour of the house. If you don't mind, Ethan."

Ethan could kiss Maggie for recognizing the need to get Zeke away from Paige. He appreciated his sister's interference and sent her a nod of approval. "It's fine by me."

"I would love a tour." Paige smiled, and Ethan's heart leapt in his chest. When she smiled his whole world brightened.

~

PAIGE RAN her hand across the cool granite. "Ethan, tell me you enjoy cooking, because this is the best kitchen I have ever seen."

Ethan's kitchen was decorated with a cozy mix of glass and stone tiles and granite countertops. A hammered copper vent hood with hanging pans was centered over the large island, the focal point of the kitchen. The back door and windows faced the lake and cast the radish-red and marmalade-orange rays of the setting sun across the stainless-steel appliances.

"I do. Cooking has always relaxed me. I learned a lot from a friend. She's the head chef in one of the top restaurants in Boston. She made sure I chose the correct appliances in case she ever visited."

Paige hoped this woman would never visit.

"You better start your tour." Ethan grabbed a plate from the fridge, piled high with burgers and bratwurst. "We'll eat in about twenty minutes."

Paige followed Maggie into the living room. She loved the vaulted tongue-and-groove ceilings and carved pillars. Paige ran her hands across the family of carved bears that helped support the grand staircase. The wide-plank wood floors shone but were toned down with rich, dark, coffee-colored plush rugs. A soft leather couch was positioned for optimal viewing pleasure in front of a large-screen television. The spectacular space was a true showcase of Maggie's skill as an interior designer. Paige reached down and petted a brown tabby cat curled up into a tight ball on the couch. The cat yawned, stretched, and exposed his belly for Paige to rub. "Who is this?"

"That's Fenway. Isn't he gorgeous?" Maggie said.

"He is." Paige stroked his soft fur. "What a perfect name."

"I remember you had a cat growing up—Lydia, right?" Maggie said.

"Good memory. Yes. Miss Lydia Bennet."

"Do you have one now?"

"No, but I'd love another," Paige said. "Someday."

They continued through the house, and Paige couldn't stop touching things. She loved the colorful accent pillows in red, orange, and blue that echoed the shades of the sky outside. She moved in circles, taking in the giant log beams and the ornate black iron railings with a pine tree motif that wrapped the upper level.

"This is stunning," Paige said.

Maggie beamed. "Thanks. I had fun and was able to showcase it as my last college project. I got an A."

"I love it. You're incredibly talented."

"I have to show you the upstairs." Maggie led her to the second level. "Don't tell Ethan I showed you his bedroom, but it's one of my favorite rooms."

The thought of entering Ethan's bedroom had Paige wishing he were the one showing her, not his sister.

As they climbed the stairs Maggie said, "I can't believe you two are dating. When did this happen?"

The way Ethan had looked at her downstairs and scowled at his brother flirting with her made her giddy. Apparently, Maggie had picked up on the chemistry between them. Paige wanted to squeal with delight. All she could think about was the kiss they shared. She took a sip of her wine and shrugged. "I'm not totally sure if we are officially dating. I mean, he kissed me the other night when we were packing the store, but we haven't really talked about it."

Maggie cheered. "You are totally dating! You're perfect for each other." Maggie set her glass on the dresser. She fell back onto the bed and laughed.

The room screamed masculinity. A king-size four-poster log

bed was the focal point of the space. Paige ran her hand across the dark-green duvet.

She set her glass next to Maggie's on the dresser. "I don't know. I'm returning to New York, so I'm not sure it's a good idea. Besides, why would Ethan be interested in me when he can have anyone he wants?"

Maggie held her hand up like a traffic cop. "Okay. Listen carefully. While my brother has women throwing themselves at him all the time, he's a one-woman kind of guy and always has been. When he's interested in someone, he's all in. Which also makes him vulnerable and easily hurt. Everyone can tell from the way he looks at you, he's definitely interested. And before you can protest further, he's interested because although you may not think so, you're beautiful, you're successful, and you have a great body, which I'm totally jealous of. And you could always move back home."

Paige appreciated Maggie's insight into Ethan's dating habits. And although she would like nothing more than to see where this relationship could go, she needed to think of her future. "There's no financial security here for me. Even if I wanted to run the bookstore, which Abe has hinted at already, I have no idea how I'd continue to keep it open."

They heard it at the same time. A soft cough. Maggie sprang to her feet. "Sorry." She fled from the room, but not before glancing over her shoulder and winking at Paige.

Ethan leaned against the doorjamb with a smile on his face. His thumbs hung from his faded jean pockets, and the snug fit of his soft, worn T-shirt showed off his muscular chest.

Paige swallowed. Hard. "So, how much of that did you hear?"

Ethan moved aside, giving her enough space to leave the room, but as she came up next to him, he stopped her. He bent down and whispered, "Almost everything, and Maggie is right."

Paige tilted her head up, her lips close to his. "Right about what, exactly?"

Ethan traced her jawline and tucked a loose strand of hair behind her ear. "You're beautiful and I'm totally into you." And then, his lips were upon her. She wrapped her arms around his waist and pulled him closer, and that was all it took for him to deepen the kiss. He tasted of blackberries and apples.

"Hey, you two, dinner's ready!" Chloe called from downstairs.

They pulled apart and Ethan rested his chin on top of Paige's head. She buried her forehead into his chest. "We definitely need to make a habit of this," he said.

Paige blushed. "I agree."

He placed a kiss on her temple. "Can I take you out sometime?"

She took a deep breath and slipped her hand into Ethan's. "I'd like that. We'd better get downstairs."

"Always the rule follower," he muttered.

She heard the chitchat and laughter coming from the kitchen before they crossed the great room. Paige looked up at Ethan, and he squeezed her hand and then let go, but directed her toward the gathering with his hand on the small of her back. When she noticed all the people with drinks in their hands and plates being passed around, she realized she had left her wine upstairs on Ethan's dresser.

Paige couldn't stop smiling. She wanted to dance, scream, squeal like a little girl. Ethan had kissed her again, and she felt it all the way to her toes.

With a smirk on his face, Zeke handed her and Ethan a plate, and they filled them with food.

Maggie came up behind her and whispered, "You go, girl." She handed Paige her wine glass, then moved into the kitchen and retrieved the wine bottle. She refilled her own glass and then, like a perfect hostess, refilled Paige's.

"Let's sit on the deck to eat, and then make our way to the lake," Ethan said.

"Perfect." Paige smiled.

FOUR WOODEN BENCHES surrounded the fire. A folded red-and-black plaid blanket rested on the empty bench. Alexis and Zeke, Garrett and Cole, and Chloe and Maggie were taking up three benches, leaving one bench open for Paige and Ethan. Paige remembered the times she'd observed the Reynolds siblings gathered around the fire, talking and laughing. She'd always yearned to be part of a large, close-knit family.

She sat, and Ethan picked up the blanket and sat next to her, spreading it over their laps.

Zeke stood and stoked the fire, adding an oak log and causing the fire to spit and spark as he moved the embers around. From what Paige could tell, Alexis and Zeke were talking about a construction job. Garrett and Cole discussed the marketing plan for Northern Lights Brewery, the business Garrett and his friend Mason owned in downtown Minneapolis.

Maggie offered Paige a tray filled with marshmallows, chocolate bars, and graham crackers. "Paige, when do you need to return to New York?"

Paige skewered a marshmallow onto a roasting stick and held it over the fire. "Between family medical leave and vacation time, I can stay until the Monday after the Fourth of July festival, but I need to attend a charity event in a few weeks."

"What kind of charity event?" Maggie asked.

Chloe blew out the flame from her burning marshmallow. "Paige runs a charity with her friend Henry."

"It's called Project Night-Light. Henry and I started it together. We hold an annual gala the third week in June—it's our biggest fundraiser."

Garrett asked, "So you raise money through ticket sales?"

"That's how we did it at first, yes, but we're serving more communities now. We now rely heavily on our silent auction."

Chloe said, "I've been donating jewelry sets for a couple years now."

"They always bring in a lot of money," Paige said. "I keep telling her she needs to sell her jewelry online."

"Yes, and I keep telling Paige that jewelry would become too much like a business, and I wouldn't have fun making it anymore."

Ethan chimed in. "I still have a lot of friends across the league. I'm guessing a few pieces of signed memorabilia would go over well."

"I'd love that, yes." Paige patted Ethan's leg.

Ethan squeezed her hand and grinned.

"I have a few furniture pieces sitting around the shop if you're interested," Cole said.

"A few?" Chloe laughed. "Cole has every nook and cranny of our grandfather's old workshop filled."

"Really? I'd love to see what you have."

"It sounds like you have a lot going on in New York. I bet you can't wait to get back." Alexis tucked her blanket underneath her and reached toward the fire to warm her hands.

Paige rotated her marshmallow stick over the fire. "Yes and no. I love the city, but I'm enjoying being home, too."

"I'm trying to talk her into staying," Chloe said.

Alexis leaned forward and stabbed at the fire with her stick. "What would you miss most about New York if you moved back here?"

"The ethnic diversity and the energy, the theatres, the museums, the food."

Chloe zipped up her sweatshirt. "But you can't beat nights like this, when the only sounds you hear are frogs, crickets, and owls, and not horns honking and sirens blaring."

"Couldn't you still be an editor and live here?" Maggie asked.

If she were to edit remotely, she'd have to start her own editing business, and that was a risk she didn't want to take until she had signed a traditional book contract for the next three books in her series. The thought of staying in Deer Creek Falls with her grandpa, Ethan, and her friends appealed to her. "The publishing firm I work for prefers their editors to work in-house." She pulled her marshmallow off the stick—perfectly soft and golden brown, just the way she liked it.

Ethan handed Paige a graham cracker with a chocolate square on it. She placed her warm marshmallow on top, and Ethan capped it with another cracker. "Thanks," she said. She bit into the gooey goodness. "Mmmm . . . it's been a long time since I had one of these."

"Have you thought of opening a coffee shop in Turner Books?" Ethan asked. "I know how much you love your coffee."

Alexis set her roasting stick down. "Um . . . I'm not sure I should say anything, but I heard there already is a coffee place coming to town. I can try to find out more."

Paige was too focused on what was happening in her own life; she should be spending more time thinking of ways to bring in money for Turner Books. A coffee shop would have been perfect. "I think that's great. New York has a coffee shop on every corner. Having one in town will make the tourists happy. I know I went through withdrawal without my daily mint mocha. Can you imagine Abe making frou-frou coffee?"

Everyone laughed.

"How's Abe doing?" Garrett said.

"He's getting around better, thanks for asking."

Garrett leaned over and opened the cooler next to him. "I brought samples of a creamy amber I'm working on. I'm thinking of calling it 'Lake Lounger.' Would anyone like to try one?"

"I would love to try one," Paige said.

Garrett sat to her left. He pulled out a chilled bottle, popped the top with an opener attached to the cooler, and handed it to her. Paige took a swig. "I think this is the best beer I've ever had!" She licked her lips.

"Okay, pass me one," Chloe said. "If Paige likes it, it must be good. I know she's a wine snob, but she only likes a handful of beers."

"If you need anyone to write a review, Garrett, I'd be happy to," Paige offered. "In the book world it's all about reviews. The more reviews, the better it sells."

"Speaking of books . . . Ethan, have you gotten a response from L.C. Brooks?" Chloe asked.

Paige stared across the fire at Chloe. Chloe smirked and took a swig from her beer. Some friend she was.

"Yes. She turned me down. Said she had family obligations and couldn't be pulled away. I hope to change her mind, though."

THOUSANDS OF STARS littered the sky. May in Minnesota still brought chilly nights. Paige and Chloe's breath hung in the air as they walked to Chloe's Jeep.

"I could have walked, but thanks for the ride." Paige shivered and pulled her coat closed.

"No problem. Besides, how else could I pump you for information?" Chloe bumped shoulders with Paige. "You and Ethan looked cozy."

"We didn't exactly have a choice. It was funny how all

benches were occupied when we arrived at the bonfire."

Chloe started the Jeep and turned the heat on high. "What's going on between you two?"

Paige wasn't ready to kiss and tell. The way Ethan gazed into her eyes before he kissed her, she knew he was interested. But she had a life in New York, not in Deer Creek Falls. Not anymore. She couldn't afford to leave her job. She was determined never to be like her mother, always moving from one man to the next or if she was between men, begging Abe for money.

"Earth to Paige."

"Hmmm?"

"You and Ethan. You seemed . . . *friendly*."

"Do you remember when my hero and heroine kissed for the first time in *Catch Me*?"

"*Yesss,*" Chloe squealed. "That good, huh?"

"Spectacular." Paige replayed the panty-melting kiss in her mind for the hundredth time.

"I can tell by the giddiness in your voice. Don't you think maybe it's time for you to come clean about L.C. Brooks? You should do the book signing."

"Watch out!" Paige grabbed for the dash and Chloe braked fast. A large doe ran across the dirt road in front of them with her fawn trailing behind her. Both deer safely reached the other side. "We don't get much wildlife in Manhattan. I'd forgotten about all the deer around here."

Chloe laughed as she pulled into Abe's driveway. "And don't forget the bear, raccoons, and coyotes."

Paige was touched to see that her grandpa had left the outside lights on for her. "I'll talk to you tomorrow, Chloe. Sweet dreams."

"Good night."

Paige got out of the Jeep, but before the car door closed Chloe yelled, "Say yes to the signing!"

It was after midnight and Paige had gotten her second wind. She checked on her grandpa; he was sound asleep. His bedside lamp was still on, a book on his chest. She removed his glasses and the latest bestselling crime novel, and set both on the nightstand. She pulled the covers over him and shut off the light. Paige poured herself a glass of wine, turned the stove light off, and headed upstairs to her childhood room.

She slipped into her favorite Red Sox jersey and soft cotton pajama pants, got under the covers, and opened her laptop. She opened an email from Henry. Attached was a meme of Fred from *Scooby Doo* pulling a hood off a ghost. "Let me see who you really are."

Paige replied to Henry, "Cute, good try, but I'm not ready yet."

With a deep breath, she attached her manuscript, sans the ending, and typed a quick message. "Thanks for keeping me on track. Give me a few days and you'll have the ending, too—I finally figured it out!! I'm attaching the final cover. It's beautiful. I hope you agree." She relaxed just a bit more and polished off her wine.

Her phone pinged. Unknown number. She opened the text message: *I had fun tonight.* Ethan. She hadn't given him her number, but she needed to thank whoever had.

She wanted to jump up and down on her bed like a giddy schoolgirl. *Me too*, she texted back.

Ethan replied right away. *We forgot to talk about the scavenger hunt. Are you available Sunday afternoon?* His text was followed by a praying-hands emoji.

She laughed before typing, *Sure.*

Great. How about 2:00? My house.

I'll be there. Smiley-face emoji.

CHAPTER NINE

*P*aige raised her hand to knock on Ethan's front door. A noise in the woods jolted her to attention. She looked left and saw a rabbit hop out from under a towering pine tree. She turned to knock again and jumped, startled to see Ethan there, smirking at her from the other side of the screen door. Good thing she wasn't a screamer; that would have been embarrassing.

"Hi, Paige." Ethan opened the door for her, and she walked in. He peeked outside, looking for something nefarious. She knew when he spotted the rabbit because he laughed. "Thank goodness it wasn't a squirrel."

"Go ahead and laugh. If I remember correctly, you're the one who squealed when the squirrel ran between your legs. Besides, it was you who startled me, not the cute bunny."

Ethan laughed. "I did, didn't I? Come on in." Ethan motioned toward the kitchen. "I whipped us up a snack."

Paige followed him into the kitchen.

"Have a seat." He gestured to a counter stool. "What can I get you to drink? Water, wine, beer?"

"Water is fine."

"Coming right up." Ethan grabbed a pitcher from the fridge. "How do you feel about lemon and cucumbers in your water?"

Paige chuckled. "Sounds perfect."

Ethan filled two glasses with ice. "Hey, no laughing."

"I didn't take you for an infused-water kind of guy."

"Well then, I guess you'll have to get to know me better."

"I guess so." If Paige was being honest with herself, she welcomed being paired with Ethan to work on festival events, though she needed to be careful not to fall head over heels for him. Although after the previous night, she might have already fallen.

Ethan set a circular cheese board fashioned from two exotic woods, on the island. The darker wood represented the stitching of a baseball.

"This looks incredible. Did Elsie stop over to help?" Paige smirked.

Ethan made the motion of a knife being thrust and twisted into his chest. "I'm shocked you would think I couldn't put a simple snack together."

She laughed. "Sorry. It's just your grandma loves to entertain. Plus, she's the ultimate matchmaker and probably thought you could use the help." Paige motioned to the display in front of her. "This is not a simple snack. A round of brie with some sort of cranberry topping? Crackers. Dried apricots. Dark chocolate truf- fles?" She popped one into her mouth. "Mmm . . . you spoil me."

"I'm happy to."

She felt surprisingly at ease with him after the delicious kiss they'd shared the day before. Would she be wrong to hope for more?

"Paige?" Ethan smirked.

"Sorry. I zoned out for a minute." She grinned shyly.

She swiveled the counter stool to face him as he moved close. Ethan parted her legs with his and looked down at her. Paige's heartbeat sped up as she gazed into his hazel eyes. He brushed his thumb under her bottom lip and lifted her chin. As he leaned down and pressed his lips against hers, all thoughts about why she was there vanished.

The back screen door slammed. "There you are—oops!" Maggie said as she entered the kitchen. Paige could feel the heat rise in her face. Ethan cleared his throat and glared at his sister.

"Sorry. I've been trying to reach you all morning. Hi, Paige. I hope I'm not intruding." Maggie grinned.

"Um, no, of course not. I came over to discuss the scavenger hunt and we were just . . . having a snack."

"Ha! Sure, a snack."

Ethan turned toward his sister. "What do you need, Maggie?"

"I've been texting you."

"I've been busy."

"I see that." Maggie grinned from ear to ear. She continued, "You said you'd help me paint Cabin Four. You should have texted me back, and then I wouldn't have interrupted."

"Sorry. I forgot. Can it wait until later tonight?"

She waved him off. "Of course. Text me when you're available. Bye, Paige."

"Bye, Maggie, see you later."

As the door sounded behind her, Paige said, "She really is lovely and talented."

"Yeah, she is." Ethan leaned in close. "So, where were we?"

Even though she wanted to pick up where they'd left off, Paige knew it would be dangerous if she allowed this relationship to blossom. Not that she'd ever had a long-distance relationship, but from what she'd heard, they didn't last.

"You promised me lunch, and we really need to plan this scavenger hunt. I'm out of my element with this event. I've never planned something like this, have you?"

Ethan stepped back. "Nope. But I've done some research and have a plan. First, though, let's eat."

PAIGE HAD CAPTURED HIS HEART. The cute way she blushed at being caught locking lips with him made things stir in him he hadn't experienced before. He enjoyed her easy, caring spirit and minimal makeup. Bridgit had been all show, all the time. Always dressed to perfection and makeup perfect, she was constantly ready in case a camera was in sight. Ethan couldn't help but fall for Paige—a dangerous thought, since she'd be leaving soon.

"My computer is in my office. I'll grab it and show you what I have in mind."

"Sure."

Fenway lounged on a chair in front of the window, enjoying the afternoon sun. Paige ran her hand over his warm fur while she waited for Ethan to return.

"You had a cat growing up, didn't you?" Ethan asked, reappearing with his laptop in his hand.

"Yep. Lydia."

"Right. *Pride and Prejudice*. Maggie mentioned your cat was named after a character in one of your favorite books."

"You remembered?"

"Of course. I remember a lot of things," he said. "How about we sit outside on the deck? I have a hard time sitting inside on a nice sunny day."

At least on the deck he could sit next to Paige on the wicker loveseat. They settled in, and he powered up his computer. "I've never participated in a scavenger hunt like we're tasked to create, but I think I have an idea." He clicked on a link to a website on how to write a scavenger hunt.

"Brilliant. I should have thought to google it."

Ethan scrolled through the web page. "There's thousands of ideas, from creating secret codes to writing clever messages or poems, word searches, you name it. But the one I like best is taking pictures. We would crop the picture to show only a small portion."

"I like that a lot. Since this is a town event, the pictures we take can show off the best features of the town." Paige stood. "I'll be right back."

When she returned, she had her notebook and pen in hand. "I thought we could make a list of the landmarks we need to visit."

He could just as easily have typed the list on his computer or in the Notes app on his phone, but Paige hadn't changed; she still carried a pocket notebook.

Ethan closed his laptop, noting the title on the front of her notebook. "'Novel Ideas,' huh?"

Paige stammered, "Oh. Novel as in new . . . a novel idea." She flipped quickly to a blank page. "Okay. I'm going to assume many of the residents will participate, but I think we need to focus on landmarks that are easy to access and any tourist can find."

"I agree. I know I'm jumping ahead here, but I've been thinking a lot about how everyone will receive the clues. How about when the teams sign up, they provide a cell phone number, then we would text them the first photo clue?" They turned in their seats to face each other, both excited about the game.

"Yes, and when they find—or think they've found—the correct landmark, they have to take a selfie in front of it and text the photo before they receive the next clue. This is going to be so much fun!"

When they finished their list of landmarks, Ethan stood and held a hand out to Paige. "Are we ready to take the pictures on our list?"

Paige checked her watch. "Wow. I didn't realize it was so late."

"Do you need to get home?"

"I should check on Grandpa. Although I came to run the bookstore, I need to spend more time with him."

Ethan trailed his hand down her arm and grasped her hand. "No worries. I understand. I have a cabin to help paint. Besides, we can take pictures on our third date. But promise me I can also take you to dinner."

"Third date? I didn't realize we were on our second date." Paige smiled.

"Mmm-hmm. Last night was our first."

"Really?"

He loved when her voice turned husky. "Yep."

"I thought it was just a friendly get-together."

"If I had my way, it would have been just the two of us."

Paige's lips parted.

Ethan bent closer. "Today was our second date." Paige swallowed, and he tucked a loose strand of hair behind her ear. He pulled her closer. She wrapped her arms around him. He could get used to having Paige in his arms.

*a*s Memorial Day weekend approached, the sun coming through the picture window helped warm Turner Books, now operating in its temporary location in the old souvenir shop. Paige typed frantically, trying to finish *Power Play*, the third book in her series. Her anxiety intensified with the increased volume of the pounding of nails and whining of saws from next door. She rubbed her temples and stared at the screen. *Deep breaths*. She needed to send the ending to Henry before the end of the long weekend.

A giggle escaped when Paige looked up to see a face plastered against the glass door's bottom pane. The cutest little boy had his nose and hands flattened on the window, a mischievous expression on his face. The mother pushed the door open slowly so her child wouldn't fall into the store.

"I'm sorry. He likes to leave handprints on every clean surface he encounters. I'd be happy to clean the window for you." The cheerful woman took her son's hand and led him to the cash register.

"No worries." Paige came around the counter and bent down in front of the little boy, a redhead with big, round blue eyes and an adorable smattering of freckles across his nose. "Hi, what's your name?"

The little boy scooted behind his mother's leg and peeked at Paige.

"This is my son Levi, and I'm Rachel." Rachel ruffled the hair on her son's head. "He's usually not this shy."

"How old are you, Levi?" Paige asked.

The little boy held up three fingers. "I like books," he said.

"Me too. You came to the right place. My name is Paige Turner. It's nice to meet you both."

"I love your name!" Rachel said.

Paige smiled. "Thank you. What can I help you find this morning?"

"I have a list."

"Great, let's see what you need." Paige scanned the list. "I have a bunch of these titles on the used-book shelf if you're interested. I'll show you where."

"That would be great." The woman followed her.

Paige pulled a few titles from the shelf and handed them to Rachel. The little boy tugged on Paige's pant leg.

"Do you have books on dogs?"

"I sure do. If your mom doesn't mind, I'll show you one of my favorites."

"Absolutely. Thank you, Paige." Rachel looked at her son. "Levi, be respectful to Miss Turner."

"I will, Mama."

Levi held out his hand for Paige. She led him to the children's section and pulled *The Pokey Little Puppy* from the book bin. Levi sat in the neon-green beanbag chair and settled in with the book. Rachel came around the corner and said, "He'll stay that way for hours if I let him."

This was the reason bookstores were needed, and the reason Paige and Henry had started their charity. The twinkle in a child's eye when they connected with a book warmed her heart. Although she'd cursed the noises coming from next door earlier, she looked forward to the renovations being complete and Ethan's vision of the kids' corner coming to life.

When Rachel sat near Levi, Paige moved back to the front counter and opened her laptop, giving them time to look through their books.

Listening to Levi read his book helped Paige relax. He invented a new story from the pictures; she found it adorable.

It wasn't long before Rachel placed several used books and a new children's book on the cash desk. Paige rang up Rachel's purchase on Abe's pride and joy, the antique till made in 1940 by National Cash Register that her great-grandfather bought for the store before Abe was born. It would be easier to use her iPad, but she loved the old register.

After Rachel and Levi left, a few more people wandered through the store, but didn't purchase anything. Paige remembered the days when the bookstore was hopping with customers during tourist season. How could Abe keep the store going with traffic patterns like this? She needed to figure out a plan of action. Maybe the stream of customers would increase over the next few weeks.

A slight breeze blew in as Abe clumsily entered the store. Paige clicked save, quickly closed her laptop, and pushed it aside. "Grandpa, what are you doing here?"

"I needed to get out of the house." Abe looked around as he struggled with his crutches. "This is a good temporary space." One crutch fell to the floor. Elsie followed him in, picked up the crutch, and handed it to him.

Paige gave her grandpa her best stink eye. "I see you recruited help."

Elsie shrugged. "What could I do? He would have tried to

walk all the way to town. He's stubborn and he's beyond reasoning with."

"Yes, he is. I think he's getting worse with age."

Abe leaned on one crutch and pointed at her. "Oh, hogwash. I've always been this way." He winked.

"Thank you for making sure he arrived safely," Paige said.

Elsie moved two chairs near the cash register. "You know what to do, old man. Take a seat. You may have convinced me to get you here, but you're still sitting with your leg raised."

"Yes, ma'am." Abe saluted her.

Elsie pulled a tin of cookies from her oversized bag and placed it next to the fresh pot of coffee on the small table to the left of the front counter.

"Chocolate chip?" Paige asked. Her stomach growled.

Elsie handed her one. "Yes. I made a batch this morning." She slipped an arm around Paige. "You look tired, dear. Not sleeping well?"

Paige had stayed up late into the night, writing. She was close to the finish line. A few more hours and she'd be typing "the end" and sending the file to Henry. "Too many ideas floating around in my head, I guess."

"Ideas?"

Paige gestured to their surroundings. "The store, the scavenger hunt, a lot of things."

"Maybe my grandson, too?"

The door opened and Maggie walked in. "Hi, Paige. I'm here to steal you away. I would love your input on lighting fixtures."

Saved by the bell. "Are they next door?"

"No, they're in my workshop."

"You two go ahead. Abe and I are happy to hold down the fort." Elsie waved them out the door.

∼

MAGGIE PULLED her car in front of a majestic red barn. If Paige remembered right, it used to be owned by a cantankerous old farmer. The area around the barn was beautifully landscaped with fieldstone and perennial grasses. A lazy stream trickled nearby. Paige pictured a romantic country wedding. Maybe she'd use the setting in her next book.

"Who owns the barn?" Paige asked.

Maggie pulled the door open and two young girls jumped out of the shadows. "Very funny, you two." Maggie caught one around the waist, and the other one burst out laughing.

"Roman owns the barn, and these are his precocious ten-year-old twin daughters, Nikki and Nora. Girls, this is Paige Turner. Abe's granddaughter. She used to tell me the best stories when I stayed over at her house."

"Really? We love stories! We're actually between books right now," Nikki said with a serious scowl.

Nora slugged her twin on the arm. "It's because you ruined the ending of my book for me, so I ruined the ending of yours." Nora shrugged like it was a natural retaliation.

"Maybe you could recommend a new book. But not now." Nikki shoved Nora. "Tag. You're it!" And they were off, chasing each other through the yard.

"They have a lot of energy. I have no idea how they sit still to read." Maggie shook her head.

"It's great they love to read. When you drop me back off at the store, I'll send a few books home with you that I know they will love."

"They'd like that. Thank you."

"Now, tell me, how can you tell them apart?" Paige asked.

"Once you get to know them, you can tell. Their personalities are very different. Nikki likes to add strands of color to her hair—Great-Aunt Emma showed her how to do it using Kool-Aid so it would be easy to wash out. Nora is more reserved. Plus, she has chubby cheeks."

Paige chuckled. "I'll remember that."

"Don't tell Nora I told you how to tell them apart." Maggie reached around the wall and flipped a switch, illuminating neatly stacked shelves full of wood, furniture, old signs, and miscellaneous items.

"Wow, you have quite the collection."

"Alexis and I started saving treasures from old homes that were being renovated or torn down. We collected so many items we needed to store them somewhere. Look, I have an entire collection of old doorknobs."

Paige picked one up and turned it around in her hand. "Be careful of these, they fall out and hold you hostage in bathrooms."

Maggie laughed. "Good to know, but I won't advertise that. Let me show you what I've been working on."

Paige followed Maggie to the back of the barn. She took in the vast collection of antiquities. An old table held vintage signs, wood boards, and paint. Paige ran a hand over an old metal coffee sign.

"I'm making a few lamps for the bookstore," Maggie said.

"You made these? They're wonderful."

Paige slid a lamp closer and lifted it to read the spines of the old books Maggie had drilled holes through. Colorful hardcovers were stacked in a pile, with a black metal stem holding the lampshade in place.

"I hope you're not offended I drilled holes through these books. My grandma brought over a box of them Abe thought I could use."

"If Gramps picked them out, I have no objections."

Maggie led her to a shelf that held a menagerie of chandeliers. "These are the two choices I thought would look good in the store." Maggie picked up the first one. "This one is an Italian chandelier circa 1930."

"I love the cascading tulips," Paige said.

"Isn't it pretty? We pulled it from a home on Summit Avenue in St. Paul. It was in rough shape, so I painted it black. I'll add bent-tip bulbs. Oh, and we have two of these, too." Maggie set the tulip fixture to the side and picked up a smaller chandelier. "This one we pulled from a home in Duluth. It's more industrial looking with the thick iron and seeded glass shades. What do you think?"

Paige pointed to the most simplistic. "I like this one."

"Oh, good. That's the one I like too. I'll tag these for you." Maggie pointed to the red toolbox next to Paige. "Can you grab the two tags sitting on top? There should be a pen in there somewhere, too."

Paige rummaged through the toolbox and pulled out a jeweled plastic ring. "This is an interesting thing to keep in a toolbox."

Maggie waved her off. "Oh, that. It's nothing. It's just a trinket from the last wedding I attended in Las Vegas."

Paige handed Maggie the tags and pen. "Ooh, is this a 'What happens in Vegas, stays in Vegas' kind of story?"

"Something like that." Maggie secured the tags onto the chandeliers.

Interesting. No doubt there was a story behind the ring, but she wouldn't push. She couldn't fault Maggie for being guarded when she herself wasn't brave enough to reveal her own secret.

"So, what about you and Ethan?" Maggie asked.

Paige smiled. "What do you mean?"

"C'mon, Paige. You and Ethan."

Paige sighed. "I don't know what to tell you. I care a lot about him."

"You know he's always liked you, right?"

Paige laughed. "I don't think so, Maggie. He barely knew I

existed in high school. We only conversed when I was with Chloe."

"No. I mean he's always had a thing for you." Maggie waved a hand in the air, "I might have been a kid, but I was pretty observant for my age."

"I think you're remembering things a bit differently. He never once showed interest in me other than as a fellow classmate, neighbor, and Cole and Chloe's friend."

"Maybe. I just remember he'd always watch you when you read by the lake or when you were swimming with Chloe. Besides, why do you think all his girlfriends look like you?"

Now Paige thought Maggie might be delusional, and she threw her head back and laughed. "I think he has a thing for blondes. That's it."

Maggie held her gaze. "Since you plan on returning to New York, which I wish you'd reconsider, please don't lead him on. I can tell you this—I haven't seen him happier in a long time. Did you know Ethan was engaged once?"

"I did. It was hard to miss, the way it was splashed all over the tabloids."

"That's the thing. When he was dating Bridgit, he appeared in tabloids like never before. The gossip rags followed them around constantly. Ethan hated all the attention. After the last concussion he suffered, Luke arrived at the hospital in time to catch Bridgit on the phone telling someone details about Ethan's injury. Luke thought she was on the phone with my mom but the next morning, those details appeared in the paper. I don't know if he was right to do it, but Luke felt compelled to let Ethan know what he'd overheard. He took it pretty hard and . . . I just don't want to see him hurt again."

"Thank you for telling me. I'm glad you did. I have no intention of hurting Ethan. I've been upfront with everyone about returning to New York, and I don't know what that means for the two of us." Paige felt sick to her stomach. Wasn't she doing the same thing Bridgit did? She wasn't one to seek attention like Bridgit obviously craved, but she wasn't being totally honest with Ethan. "I appreciate you sharing your concern, but please give us time to figure this out."

"I can do that. You'll be at Chloe's tonight, right?"

"I wouldn't miss it."

CHAPTER ELEVEN

*P*aige parked in the alley behind Rural Chic Boutique, climbed the old wooden steps to Chloe's apartment above, and knocked.

Chloe yelled, "Come in!"

Laughter filled the kitchen. Maggie, Alexis, and Chloe stood around the island. Paige held up the two items she carried. "I brought wine and chocolate."

"My two favorite things," Chloe said.

A plethora of snacks covered the countertop. Alexis set out plates and napkins.

The oven timer buzzed, and Chloe removed a cake pan filled to the brim with her legendary loaded mac and cheese.

"I'm so not going to fit into my clothes when I get home." Paige set the bottle of Riesling she'd brought on the counter.

"Here, try this." Maggie handed her a glass filled with a brownish slushy mix.

Paige sniffed it and sipped. "Wow, that's good, what is it?"

"Alexis's signature drink, Brandy Slush."

"I'll need the recipe for this one." Paige took another sip.

"Don't drink them too fast, they'll sneak up on you." Chloe

placed a serving spoon in the mac and cheese. "Okay, dig in everyone, you lightweights need food."

They finished filling their plates and moved to the living room. Alexis sat cross-legged on the sofa. "Okay, Paige, time to share. You and Ethan are the biggest news to hit Deer Creek Falls in a long time."

In a sing-song voice and holding an empty glass, Maggie sang, "K-I-S-S-I-N-G."

"How old are you?" Alexis laughed and threw a bun at Maggie, hitting her in the head.

"Hey!"

Paige laughed at the antics between the best friends.

Chloe smirked behind her glass. "Well . . . there probably *is* bigger news, it just hasn't been *revealed* yet."

Alexis and Maggie stared and waited for one of them to say something. Paige glared at Chloe.

Chloe had been trying to get her to tell everyone she was L.C. Brooks, but she wasn't ready yet. She only had another month until she returned to New York, and then nobody would be the wiser.

"You should ask Ethan to the charity gala," Chloe said, trying to cover her faux pas.

"You should!" Alexis and Maggie said in unison.

Paige took another drink. "I don't know, do you think he'd want to go?"

"Oh, he'll go. I have a feeling he'd follow you anywhere," Maggie said.

Chloe and Alexis both nodded.

"How about we all head downstairs and help you choose a gown?" Chloe said.

Maggie clapped her hands together. "Ooh, yes, let's!"

"First things first," Alexis declared. "Some of us need to eat more so we don't get too looped. And we don't want to waste this delicious food. Paige can fill us in on the gala and on her newly formed relationship with Ethan." She held her glass in the air to toast the group.

Alexis was the logical one, always thinking and planning. They each refilled their plates and glasses, and Paige gave them the rundown on the charity gala.

The girls wanted more details about Ethan. Where did they first kiss? How was it? Although some questions were embarrassing, Paige felt herself relax with these amazing women. How was she ever going to return to New York? She was building strong connections with Maggie and Alexis, and the thought of leaving Chloe again was unbearable.

When she wasn't joining in on the silly banter about horrible first dates, disastrous entanglements, unruly seniors, and café mishaps, Paige was listening intently and watching the facial expressions of her friends for book-worthy material. Like the writer she was, Paige listened and learned.

Alexis gathered the empty plates, and Maggie announced it was time to head downstairs and try on dresses. Single file, they made their way down the narrow wooden steps into Rural Chic Boutique. Chloe flipped the light switch then turned on a 1980s rock station. The boutique reflected Chloe's eclectic style, with elegant ball gowns in one corner and a wall of concert tees in another. Racks made of wood and black industrial pipe held clothes for both men and women. Near the register was a rack of purses and tote bags made from recycled grain and coffee bags. The store smelled of lavender and leather.

Paige ran her hand across the gowns. The elegance of the satin, lace, and beads had her shaking her head in disbelief. The gowns weren't regular ball gowns, but were enhanced with mixed-media embellishments. Some had antique keys to fasten a strap or sash, while others had fine chains that swooped down in the back.

"What do you think?" Chloe asked.

Paige fingered the material and gently slid aside each gown on the rack to look at the next one. Occasionally she'd lift the full skirts and fan them out in front of her. "Wow! How did I not know you were making these?"

Chloe shrugged. "It's a new line. My mom is responsible for all of this. She wanted to reuse one of her dresses but didn't want anyone to know. I embellished it, and she got more compliments on it than she did with the old one."

"You do realize you could make a fortune selling your custom dresses in New York, don't you?"

Chloe punched her on the arm. "Yeah, right."

"I'm not kidding, Chloe. You need to market these on your website. Do you have any cards I can take with me to the gala?"

"Sure, but I doubt the hoity and toity would ever order from someone in Minnesota," Chloe said.

Maggie and Alexis headed to the dressing rooms with three dresses each.

"I'm serious. I can't wait to wear one of your creations, and I want to have cards with me when all the women start asking who designed my dress."

"Well then, you'd better try one on."

Maggie exited the changing room and struck a pose in front of the large three-paneled mirror. "As much as I love this dress, I think it would look better on you, Paige."

"I'd love to try it on."

"I'll be right back." Maggie hurried back into the dressing room.

The girls were waiting for Paige when she appeared in the floor-length buttery-yellow dress. Chloe smoothed and gathered the dress in a few places.

Alexis handed her a pair of heels. "Ethan won't be able to keep his hands off you."

Secretly, Paige hoped he wouldn't.

Maggie looked over her shoulder as she placed dresses back on the rack. "When will you ask Ethan to the gala?"

Chloe handed her a pair of earrings. "You need to ask him. He'd probably book first-class tickets if you let him make the plans."

Paige turned to admire the open back. "Should I try on another dress or do you like this one?"

"That one," Maggie and Alexis said in unison.

"That's definitely the one," Chloe agreed. "I'd like to take in the waist and the shoulders a bit. I'll have it ready for you by the end of the day tomorrow." Chloe reached for her pins and did some pulling and tucking. "Okay. Go ahead and take it off."

CHAPTER TWELVE

*E*than was dead on his feet. He'd thought he was in good shape until he started back at Reynolds and Sons. He'd been helping Roman and his crew landscape a new lake home on the north end of Balsam Lake. They'd excavated the backyard, creating steps to the lake using large limestone slabs. Once the hardscape was laid, they planted trees, shrubs, native grasses, and perennials. Ethan hadn't seen Paige all week. They'd texted, but it didn't compare to seeing her face-to-face.

His phone chirped. A text from Roman.

Don't need you tomorrow. Rest up, old man.

Perfect. He'd used muscles he hadn't used for a while, and his body needed time to recover.

He texted Paige. *Are you free tomorrow morning? Photos of landmarks?*

He waited for the three dots to disappear. *Sure. 9 a.m.?*

I'll pick you up.

With a smile on his face, he slipped his phone back into his pocket and drove to town.

The dinner rush at Rosie's Café was in full swing when he walked in. He waved to a few people before approaching the front counter. His grandma Elsie and great-aunt Emma were chatting with Rosie at the cash register. His stomach growled from the smell of hamburgers and fried onions.

"Hi, honey," his grandma said.

"Hi Gram, Aunt Emma. Hi Rosie."

"Well, don't you look tired? Let me go see if your order is ready."

"Thanks."

Rosie scurried toward the kitchen.

"I heard you and Paige shared a kiss the night of the bonfire." Emma grinned.

Ethan ran a hand through his hair. "How do you know that?"

He didn't need people in his hometown to report on his comings and goings. He'd expected the reporting to stop once he left the major leagues. He guessed it was posted on the Town Talk app. He'd been trying to figure out who created the app since he got to town, but if anyone knew, they weren't talking.

"You've forgotten how small towns work," his grandma said.

Sweaty and tired, Ethan didn't want to discuss it any longer. He thought he'd gotten away from the tabloids for good, and instead Town Talk was taking their place. He hoped it wasn't Paige who posted about their kiss. He wanted to get home to Fenway, crack open a beer, and eat his dinner.

Ethan was afraid of what was coming when Elsie and Emma glanced at each other. His siblings called it twin-speak when they shared "the look."

With a sly smile Emma said, "Honey, maybe it's time you put the app on your phone. If you're going around kissing girls, you may want to know what's being said about you."

"I only plan on kissing one girl."

His grandma rested a hand on his arm. "I adore Paige. You make such a cute couple."

Rosie handed the brown paper bag to Ethan and rang up his

order. He reached into his pocket for his wallet and handed her cash. "Keep the change."

"Thanks, hon."

Before he could escape, his grandma reached for his hand. "Has there been any progress in getting the author?"

"I've been in contact, and I'm hopeful she'll show."

Elsie reached into her tote, pulled out a book, and handed it to Ethan. "Read this and you'll get your author."

"You're kidding. *Catch Me*? Romance really isn't my genre of choice."

"I don't care. Read it—tonight."

"You don't want to let Paige down," Emma said.

Rosie nodded. "We won't tell."

He took the book. Ethan wouldn't be surprised if his reading material was reported on the Town Talk app by daybreak.

WHEN ETHAN ENTERED HIS HOUSE, Fenway stood on the small wooden entry table, awaiting his arrival. "Hey, buddy. You hungry?"

Fenway meowed.

"Me too." Ethan tossed the book, mail, and his keys down. Fenway jumped off the table and raced in front of him to the kitchen. He placed his takeout order in the microwave and opened a can of cat food. Fenway weaved between his legs as Ethan scooped a large portion of liver and chicken pâté into the cat's dish.

He slid out a kitchen chair, sat, and pulled off his boots. "I'm getting too old for this." Fenway ignored him, and Ethan headed for the shower.

When he reentered the kitchen, Fenway was back on the entry table, sitting on the book. Ever since Ethan rescued him, Fenway had had this weird obsession with sitting on things. Ethan could place a piece of paper in the middle of the living room and Fenway would sit on it. He was a strange cat, but he was great company and it didn't take much to make him happy.

Ethan transferred his dinner onto a plate. A Post-it note, attached to a clear container with a dozen white-chocolate macadamia cookies in it, read, "Enjoy the cookies." He had to remember to thank Rosie. Ethan ate two while his dinner warmed in the microwave.

Finally relaxed in his favorite chair, Ethan enjoyed Rosie's mouthwatering chicken-fried steak. He finished off his second beer and took his empty plate to the kitchen. Fenway ran in front of him, leaped onto the entry table, and resumed his position on the book. He pawed it, trying to open the cover. Ethan smiled. "Buddy, you can't open the book while sitting on it." Fenway stared at him. "I'm not reading it tonight. I'm too tired." He was glad no one witnessed the exchange between him and his cat. He could see the post now: *Ethan Reynolds has lost it. Retirement has driven him mad.*

"Fine. Move." Fenway stepped off the book and pawed him in the chest. Ethan shook his head. "I'll start it, but I'll probably fall asleep."

He returned to his chair and cracked open the book. The book was dedicated to L.C. Brooks's grandparents, who'd instilled the love of reading.

Fenway jumped onto his lap, turned around a few times, and fell asleep. It figured. Ethan thought the first paragraph would put him to sleep, but he was wrong. When he became sore from sitting in the same position, he glanced at the clock above the fireplace. He'd been reading for over four hours.

Ethan used a tissue to mark his spot and placed the book on the table. He picked up Fenway and headed for the bedroom. Being lost in a book hadn't happened to him since he read the

Harry Potter series. No wonder the women loved this author. He'd found himself laughing out loud more than once. Ethan was convinced, now more than ever, that this author would bring people into town and through the door of the bookstore. He had less than a week to convince L.C. Brooks to visit Deer Creek Falls so he could start a social media campaign. He'd try to read more before he picked Paige up in the morning. She'd mentioned she'd read it, and it had been a long time since he discussed a book with someone. He'd bring it up while they were out. Ethan sent a quick email to L.C. Brooks and fell asleep.

CHAPTER THIRTEEN

*F*riday wasn't the best day of the week to run around town taking photographs without people noticing, but Ethan didn't want to wait a day more to see Paige. He hoped most of the tourists were out on the lake or busy enjoying breakfast.

Paige waved from the porch as he pulled into the driveaway. Her long blonde hair was pulled into a ponytail, leaving the long column of her neck exposed. She wore a "The Book Was Better" V-neck tee in a shade of yellow that intensified her chocolatey brown eyes, and a pair of jean shorts that accentuated her long, toned legs.

"Good morning," she said as she climbed into his truck and buckled herself in.

Ethan leaned over and kissed her. "I've missed you."

"I've missed you too."

"Is Abe okay watching the store today?"

"Your grandma and my grandpa are both watching the store today. They've been spending a lot of time together lately." Paige waggled her brows.

"Huh. How about that." Ethan smiled and shifted into reverse.

"I thought we'd start at the fountain in town. Not too many people should be walking around since the shops don't open until ten."

"Perfect."

Ethan had always loved the fountain. A local artist had created the ten-foot bronze statue of a family of white-tailed deer running through a creek bed. It stood in front of the Deer Creek Lodge, close to the center of town.

Ethan parked in front of the lodge.

As they walked to the fountain, they waved to the boaters waiting to launch. The sun in the cloudless sky reflected off the fountain, making the statue glow.

"Let's take a selfie in front of the fountain," he said as he removed his phone from his pocket. He pulled her close, and Paige snuggled into him.

"Can you send it to me?" Paige asked.

"You bet." He tapped his screen a few times and her phone chirped.

"Thanks."

"Let's take a shot or two of the entire structure, then some close-ups. Chloe can work her magic and find us a portion we can use as the clue," Ethan said.

"Sounds like a plan."

"What's next on our list?"

"We can walk down Main, then cut over onto Lake Street to get the rest of the photos in town. I want to get a shot of the mallard hidden in the stained-glass window at the hardware store."

"The old First State Bank is on the way. We'll get a photo of the stonework."

As they walked down Main Street, he pointed to a lamppost bearing the poster advertising the author signing. "I started reading *Catch Me*."

. . .

Paige forced herself not to go into full-blown panic mode. "Really?" I wouldn't have thought of you as a romance reading kind of guy."

"It's actually really good, but don't tell anyone or I'll deny it." A hint of dimple showed when he smiled.

"Your secret is safe with me."

"I'd forgotten Chloe had mentioned it was about a pro-baseball player, a catcher. At times I felt as if I were reading about my life." Ethan laughed.

Paige drew from her years of yoga and took a deep, calming breath. "I'm guessing stories about loving baseball and the struggles making it to the big leagues are similar." *Think, Paige.* "It's the same with writers when they're asked about how they got started. The answers are almost always the same. Most talk about loving to write in grade school. It's the later years that differ. Some pursue writing, some revisit their passion later in life after kids are grown."

Ethan took her hand in his and they entwined fingers. "Yeah, you're right. For the most part, we all start out in T-ball. I was that scrawny kid."

"Scrawny kid?" Paige knew exactly which part of the book Ethan referred to.

"I was the scrawny kid adjusting my glasses and trying to hit the ball, only to miss it over and over again. I wasn't asked to be part of the T-ball team, either. The way the author described it . . . it was as if I were reliving that moment again."

Paige saw a moment of sadness flash in Ethan's eyes as he described what she'd written. She squeezed his hand. Paige remembered Abe handing Ethan *The Little Engine That Could* and telling him that with practice and determination, he'd grow up to be an excellent baseball player. The next day, she'd watched from the shadows of a pine tree as six-year-old Ethan practiced hitting the ball repeatedly.

"Come on, let's get a photo of the old Coca-Cola advertisement on the side of Mane Attraction before people catch us," Ethan said.

Paige took her phone out of her back pocket. "Stand there and I'll take your picture." She loved the faded advertisement painted high on the redbrick building of the hair salon. She snapped a picture of the sign then quickly focused on Ethan. He leaned against the brick wall with his hands in his pockets, causing his shorts to hang low on his hips. She snapped a few more. Swoonworthy.

They crossed Main Street in front of Turner Books after stopping in to talk to Elsie and Abe. Elsie liked the idea they were working on the scavenger hunt. She suggested several landmarks that were on their list and thought it would be a good idea to take a drive to the falls. Paige and Ethan laughed at her lack of subtlety. The Deer Creek Falls were a known destination for the teenagers, a place to park and have fun.

"My grandpa mentioned that the kiss we shared showed up on the Town Talk app last night."

"Yeah, I heard that too. I hoped it wasn't you."

Paige stopped walking and turned to face Ethan. "I would never post something like that on social media for all the town to see."

Ethan pulled her close. "Thank you, and I'm sorry I suspected you. That leaves Maggie. I'll have a talk with her."

Paige shook her head. "It could have been Chloe or Alexis. I did tell them about our kiss when we hung out the other night."

"Let's forget about it. I'm blowing it way out of proportion. Having my grandma tell me brought back bad memories. One of the reasons my last relationship ended was because everything we did together showed up in the tabloids." Ethan placed a quick kiss on her cheek. "Let's keep going."

Several families emerged from Rosie's Café after having a

late breakfast. The downtown area only had two stoplights, and during tourist season they were needed. A line of traffic packed the roads as far as you could see. Cars hauling compact pop-up trailers, family-filled SUVs pulling boats, recreational vehicles, and Jet Skis. Encroaching on noon, Paige and Ethan needed to wrap up their photos in town and finish with the trails.

Ethan made sure he was walking on the side of traffic as they skirted around window shoppers. Paige posed next to the stained-glass window of the hardware store. "I don't think we need to worry about anyone watching us. I don't recognize anyone."

"You can never be too sure. Smile," Ethan said. "Got it. Let's make our way down Lake and stop at the bank. That should be it for the pictures in town."

The smell of fried food from the Eagle's Nest had their stomachs grumbling.

They held hands as they made their way back to the truck. "How about an ice-cream cone?" Ethan asked.

"I'll never turn down ice cream."

The line in front of Cup and Cone wrapped around the corner, but the decadent homemade ice cream was well worth the wait. The locals referred to their small stand as 'The Hut' and was everyone's favorite.

When they were next in line, Ethan removed his wallet from his pocket.

Paige swatted his arm. "Put your money away. This one is on me."

"No way, I've got this."

Paige inched closer to the window. "Too bad. I owe you a cone."

"How do you figure?"

"When I was eight, I was here with my grandpa. I was sad because my mom had showed up for a couple of days with a new man, then left again, so my grandpa took me out for an ice-cream cone to cheer me up. I took one lick and the scoop fell to the ground. I cried, and you handed me yours."

"I remember. You freaked me out when you started crying. I always hated when Maggie cried; I'd give her anything so she'd stop. She had me wrapped around her finger."

Paige laughed. "I'm sorry I freaked you out, but it was sweet, nonetheless."

They stepped up to the window and she ordered the flavor of the day. "A double scoop of Blueberry Cheesecake for me—in a cup, please."

Ethan scanned the menu. "And I'll take a double scoop of the Peanut Butter Nutty Bar in a waffle cone."

Instead of sitting at one of the picnic tables outside the hut, they decided to stroll along the lake. They walked until they reached one of the honoree benches the beautification society raised money for. "Have you seen your grandmother's bench yet?" Ethan asked.

"Grandpa sent me a picture when it was installed."

When they reached her grandmother's bench, a man was sitting there, reading the *Lake Times* and soaking up the sun with his black lab beside him. The gold plaque fastened to the back of the bench read, "In Memory of Caroline Brooks-Turner."

The tear that escaped caught Paige off guard. Her grandmother had been gone a long time, but some days it hit her harder than others. Seeing the bench in person brought back a flood of memories. The cooking and sewing lessons, and singing from her grandmother's personal songbook.

Ethan squeezed her hand. "Are you okay?"

"Yeah. Sorry."

"There's no need to apologize. I get it. Some memories pop up when you least expect them." Ethan pointed to a vacant bench in the shade under an old oak tree. "Let's sit in the shade before our ice cream melts."

Paige enjoyed Ethan's company as they sat in comfortable silence finishing their treat, until her phone blared with an unfamiliar ringtone: "*Pa-per-back wri-ter . . . writer . . . writer . . .*" What the—? She was going to strangle Chloe.

"That's an interesting choice. I didn't know you were a Beatles fan."

"I'm not. I mean . . . I like the Beatles, but . . . Chloe must have gotten ahold of my phone." She quickly turned it off.

Ethan chuckled.

Before heading back to the truck, Ethan took a picture of the trail sign—the last of their photos. "What are your plans tonight?" he asked.

"Funny you should ask. Abe gave me the night off. Said he felt good enough to have dinner with a friend."

"How about dinner at my place—just the two of us this time?"

"It's a date."

CHAPTER FOURTEEN

*E*than dropped Paige off at home after they completed their photo-taking mission, and they agreed that Paige would send the pictures to Chloe before coming to dinner. Ethan couldn't stop smiling. He'd never wanted to spend as much time with someone as he did with Paige. He wanted to take her to his favorite places and visit hers. He wanted to find out her likes and dislikes and what made her happy. He wanted to hear her opinions and her thoughts.

He'd just started preparing dinner when there was a knock at the door. Paige wasn't expected to arrive for another hour. He wiped his hands on a towel and looked around the corner to find Cole on the other side of the screen door.

"Hey, Cole."

Cole walked into the kitchen. "Hey, I didn't think you'd be home. I'm just dropping off your chainsaw. Thanks for letting me borrow it. My replacement arrives tomorrow."

"No problem."

Ethan reached for an onion and a knife and started chopping.

Cole reached into the bowl of mixed nuts on the kitchen

island and popped a cashew into his mouth. "What are you making?"

"Meatloaf with tomato relish."

Cole sat on the counter stool and watched Ethan work. "What's the occasion?"

"Paige is coming for dinner." Ethan retrieved the fresh green beans from the fridge and set the colander in front of Cole. "Here, make yourself useful."

Cole started snapping the ends off the beans. "Don't get me wrong, I like Paige, but do you think it's wise to start a long-distance relationship? The number of times she's been home in the last ten years I can count on one hand."

Ethan tore some flat-leaf parsley off the bunch and ran his knife through the greens, then started dicing the tomatoes. Cole always had his back, and he knew his friend was looking out for him. Ethan set the knife down and placed his hands on the island. "I know it's a long shot. But, shouldn't I at least try? I was thinking of contacting my agent, seeing if there was something on the east coast. Maybe a commentator position."

"What about this place?" Cole gestured to their surroundings. "You built your dream home to be closer to your family. To start your own family."

Ethan crossed his arms. "Yeah, you're right. But Paige is different than any woman I've ever dated."

Being on the road wasn't all fun and games. There were times he dreamt of home, settling down, and starting a family. The one thing that gave him the extra push to retire was to settle back in his hometown. Granted, he'd envisioned Bridgit joining him at the time and had built the house to start a family, but things changed. Being with friends and family again felt right. Would he be okay with uprooting his new life? Something he'd yearned for, for so many years?

Cole slapped him on the back. "I don't envy you. But be careful. It sucks when you uproot your life for someone and then it doesn't work out. Maybe it will work out and you'll enjoy spending time on the road again. Shoot, I placed a bet you'd be back on the east coast within a year of your return." Cole moved to the sink, rinsed the green beans, and set them aside.

Ethan looked to his friend. "I suppose other people are betting on my life," Ethan said with a sneer.

"There may have been discussion around the family dinner table. I said you'd find a way to start the season one way or another. I lost that bet." Cole dried his hands on a towel and picked up Ethan's copy of *Catch Me*. "Wow. You must have it bad if you're reading romance."

Ethan swiped the book from Cole's hand and tossed it onto the built-in desk to the right of him. "Not a word. It's research."

"Okay—?"

Ethan went back to meal prep. He poured a bit of olive oil into a skillet and added the onions, garlic, and bay leaves to caramelize them. "Do you know the author?"

"Why would I know the author?" Cole asked.

Ethan turned from the stove. "L.C. Brooks. Does the name sound familiar?"

"Nope." Cole picked a few more cashews out of the bowl and popped them into his mouth. "Why? Should it?"

Ethan shook his head. "No, I guess not." He added peppers, parsley, and tomatoes to the pan. He couldn't pinpoint any one thing, but all the little things . . . "Do you think Paige could be the author?"

"Seriously? What makes you think that?"

"*Catch Me* is about a baseball player, a catcher, and there are scenes in the book that are similar to my life."

Cole laughed. "Wow, got much of an ego?"

"Ha ha. Forget I said anything."

Paige couldn't be the author; she would have told him by now.

There was no reason to keep it a secret. Besides, he hadn't finished the book yet. Maybe the similarities were just a coincidence.

He put ground beef and pork, eggs, and half the tomato relish into a bowl and mixed it with his hands. He needed to get the meatloaf into the oven before Paige arrived, and he still had to boil the potatoes and steam the green beans. Paige liked to eat and he loved that about her. She wasn't the kind of woman who ate a few bites and raved how delicious her meal was, only to move the rest of the food around on her plate to make it look like she'd eaten.

Cole stood up to go. "I'll head out and let you get ready for your big date."

"Thanks, Cole. I'll see you tomorrow at the softball game."

With the potatoes and green beans done, Ethan set the table. The doorbell rang, and with a smile on his face, he went to answer it.

Ethan opened the door to Paige. "Hi." She walked in, and he pulled her close. He placed one hand on the small of her back, the other tilted her chin up, and their lips met. She melted into him and the kiss deepened.

Her phone chirped with an incoming email, interrupting them. "Sorry." She pulled out her phone, frowned, and silenced it.

"Is something wrong?"

"No. I just have a lot on my mind."

Ethan frowned. "Anything I can do to help?"

"Dinner smells wonderful. All I need right now is good company and good food."

Ethan closed the door behind them and led her into the kitchen. "You're in luck, because dinner is almost ready. I hope you like meatloaf, mashed potatoes, and green beans."

"Mmm, comfort food. Perfect."

"How about a glass of wine?" Two glasses and a bottle of red stood waiting on the island.

"I would love one. Thank you."

Knowing that her time in Deer Creek Falls was limited, Paige wanted to make the best of their time together. When the moment was right, she'd break the news to Ethan. Until then, she'd enjoy the way his eyes skimmed over her body. He made her feel sexy, and glad she'd worn her black lace lingerie. Not that she thought she'd get lucky, but she hoped to reach second base. Paige could feel the spark between them. Was that love? She'd never felt that connection with Allen. She stepped toward Ethan and ran her hands under his shirt.

"Paige, you're driving me crazy," Ethan murmured. He slipped his hands under her shirt and cupped her breasts, kissing her with passion and taking her breath away as he backed her into the island. The oven timer buzzed, and he rested his forehead against hers and let out a frustrated breath. "Dinner's ready."

Paige bit her lower lip and gave Ethan her best seductive look. "I'm hungry."

He pulled her close and their tongues tangled briefly once more before he ended the kiss and then removed the meatloaf before it burned. Her eyes roamed over Ethan's strong arms and cute butt as he bent down to pull the food out of the oven.

"You know, if you keep staring at me like that, we'll never eat." Ethan smiled mischievously. He turned to pull plates from the cupboard. While Paige waited, she pulled the phone from her back pocket and quickly scanned her emails. One from Fenway11:

DEAR L.C. BROOKS,

I'm not giving up on you. The posters are made. Please don't

disappoint your readers. I promise the signing will be well worth
your time.

Yours truly,
Ethan

HER PALMS STARTED TO SWEAT. *No way.* She looked to Ethan as
he plated the food. He couldn't have figured it out.

"Anything interesting?"

He smiled his tantalizing, thousand-megawatt smile. She put
her phone back in her pocket. "I don't know yet. What can I do to
help?"

"Why don't you grab the silverware?" Ethan pointed to the
drawer next to him.

The food Ethan placed on their plates made her mouth water.
"That looks amazing."

He brought the full plates to the kitchen table, and she
followed with their wine glasses.

"Are you still wrapping up some work?" He gestured to her
phone, which she'd set face down on the table.

"It seems I can't get away from it." She took a forkful of
mashed potatoes and meatloaf. "Ethan, this is delicious. You can
cook for me anytime."

"It would be my pleasure."

There was that smile again. The smile that made her hope for
more than dinner. His hazel eyes danced with desire as he kept a
steady gaze on her.

Conversation flowed as they talked about the scavenger hunt
and their families. Paige was thankful the bookstore wasn't
brought up, because she dreaded the talk they needed to have.

"Thank you for dinner. You've spoiled plain old meatloaf for
me, the tomato relish was to die for."

"I'm glad you liked it."

"Remember I mentioned that I need to fly home and attend the charity gala? Would you want to accompany me? You can say no. I'd understand if—"

"I thought you'd never ask. I'd love to."

"You would?"

"Of course." Ethan reached across the table and placed his hand over hers. "I enjoy spending time with you. You're the last thing I think about at night and the first person I think of in the morning."

Whew. Was it hot or was she about to spontaneously combust? To hear Ethan say out loud what she'd been thinking for a while now made her long to be with him, chucking her career if that's what it took.

After Ethan's heartfelt confession she needed to confide in him or she might burst. Paige set down her fork, finished off her wine, and placed her hands on her lap. She bowed her head. "Ethan, there's a good chance we'll need to close the store at the end of the season." She met his gaze. "Before coming here tonight, Abe and I had a heart-to-heart about the future of Turner Books." With reluctance she continued, "I've been playing around with some ideas to keep the store open, but I wanted to let you know that it might not be enough." Paige tried to swallow the lump in her throat. "I'm sorry, Ethan. It was so kind and generous of you to buy the building and remodel it to our specifications. I feel like a failure, like I let you and my grandpa down."

With the back of her hand, she swiped at the tears that fell. He stood and pulled her into his arms, placing a finger under her chin. "You are an intelligent and caring person, and I respect the hell out of you. You are not a failure. I never want to hear you put yourself down." He kissed the top of her head as he wrapped her in a loving embrace. She let the tears flow.

After several minutes, she took a deep breath and placed a hand on Ethan's muscular chest. "I'm sorry I ruined the evening."

"You didn't. I get to hold you in my arms, don't I?" Ethan smiled and wiped a tear from her face with his thumb. "Although I hope the bookstore will remain open, if it can't, I know you won't come to that decision easily. I'll never regret buying the building, because it allowed me to work closely with you," Ethan said. "How's Abe doing?"

"I know he's disappointed, but he's being strong for me. He told me he's looking forward to retiring." Paige fiddled with her napkin. "Enough about the bookstore. Let's salvage this evening by watching a movie."

"Sounds good, but if you want to talk, I'm here."

Paige smiled and began clearing away the dinner plates. "Thank you."

"Leave the dishes." Ethan took the plates from her and set them by the sink. "Let's pick out a movie."

They cuddled on the couch as they settled in to watch *Iron Man*.

They talked through the first movie, ate popcorn, and made out like teenagers through the next. Neither of them were ready to take it to the next level, so clothes stayed on for the most part.

Paige woke when Fenway jumped onto her shoulder.

They'd fallen asleep on Ethan's couch. She nudged Fenway, who stretched and relocated to Ethan's side. She managed to untangle herself from Ethan's arms without waking him, then stood and adjusted her clothing. She shut the television off and tiptoed to the door. It was one o'clock in the morning, and she needed to get some shut-eye. Paige had a few things to take care of at the bookstore in the morning before heading to the charity softball game.

CHAPTER FIFTEEN

A powerful stream of water hit Ethan's face. He dodged another strike and landed on the floor, his blankets wrapped around his legs. The cold water had interrupted his dream of Paige, caressing—

Roman stood over him, a Super Soaker in his hand and a grin on his face.

"What the hell?" Ethan scrambled to stand as he unwrapped the sheet.

"We have a game in twenty minutes. I've been trying to call you. I found your phone on the counter downstairs. Get dressed."

"Game?" Ethan raked a hand through his hair. He looked around his room and it all came back to him. *Why did I give my family a key to my house?*

"Yeah, little brother. The whole town will be there to watch."

Ethan had taken a cold shower before retiring to his room after waking up on the couch alone. He and Paige had managed to carry on like lovesick teenagers, and he'd hoped she would stay the night, but she ran off before he could ask.

Roman had suckered him into playing in a charity softball game that would benefit his daughters' summer softball team, which he coached. The money raised would fund the summer league. Ethan had offered to pay for new uniforms and equipment, but Roman refused and said he wanted to set a good example for his girls. Ethan agreed. They'd had to work for their money growing up.

Ethan pulled on his uniform, jogged down the steps and sprinted into the kitchen, where Roman handed him a thermos of coffee and opened the door for him. "I threw your gear in the truck."

"Thanks." He took a sip of the strong black coffee.

As they approached the park, cars lined both sides of the gravel road for as far as they could see. "Holy crap, I guess you'll be getting those new uniforms plus equipment," Ethan said as he watched swarms of people walking along the road with lawn chairs in hand.

Roman glanced over and smacked him in the leg. "Thanks to you, little brother."

Ethan looked for Paige's Mustang but didn't see it. He hadn't stopped thinking of her since she'd left the night before.

"We're here. Are you going to get out of the truck?"

"Oh. Yeah. Sorry. Just thinking."

Roman grinned from ear to ear. "I bet you were."

Ethan downed his coffee and set the empty thermos in the cup holder. He really needed to focus. He grabbed his equipment bag from the back and made his way to the dugout.

"So, are you and Paige official?" Roman elbowed him in the side.

"How the hell do you know about that?"

"Really? You have to ask?"

Town Talk. Of course. Ethan glanced at the bleachers, waved to Rosie and her husband, and quickly perused the crowd for Paige. Sitting with their teammates, Nikki and Nora waved. He hadn't seen a crowd like this since his last high-school game before he left for the pros. People were spread over the grounds on blankets, some with picnic baskets, and a food truck painted in vibrant colors sold tacos. A large sign stretched across the back of the truck: "All proceeds going to youth sports."

"Hey, Ethan. Glad you could make it." Chloe smirked and reached for her glove. She headed for second base. She turned and yelled, "Maybe you want to play second base, since you're so familiar with it?"

Ethan sat on the bench to get his gear on and yelled, "Funny, Reid. I did catch a good one."

Chloe yelled back, "You better believe it, Reynolds."

This was what summer was all about. Baseball—or in this case softball. He strapped on his pads and looked around at the aging dugout. The old weathered wood benches had seen better days. Ethan was afraid to move; he might end up with a splinter in his ass.

One by one his teammates slapped him on the back as they headed for the field to take their positions. The pitcher, who sat next to him, placed the ball in his glove. "Let's go, we're up." They took the field.

Ethan kept an eye on the crowd, glancing at the bleachers, still looking for Paige.

He knew his pitcher could pitch. He had played on the town league with him his first year back. But this was different. Ethan had never caught a neon-green softball. At least he couldn't miss it.

The umpire came onto the field and yelled, "Play ball!" Ethan turned to see Mario in full umpire gear. Paige walked up to the batter's box.

"Make your grandpa proud. Hit it out of the park," Mario said.

"Thanks, Mario," she said.

Ethan looked up at her. "You're playing on the other team? I didn't think you played softball."

"What gave you that idea?"

Paige took her stance and waited for the pitcher.

Ethan gave a few hand signals and squared up. The pitcher looked confused and let it fly.

"Steee-riiike!" Mario shouted. Paige looked back at the ump, hand on hip.

"That was clearly ball one."

Ethan had to stand to catch the ball, and now he threw it back to the pitcher. He liked that Paige showed spunk.

"Sorry about that. I'll do better," Mario said.

Paige took her batting stance and wiggled her butt as she waited for the next pitch. What was she trying to do to him? Ethan's eyes were focused on her cute bottom one minute and the next, he found himself looking up at a cloudless blue sky.

He heard the crowd gasp and Paige knelt, grasping his bicep. "Ethan, are you okay?"

The pitcher stood over him, running his hands through his hair, clearly nervous. Roman ran in from third base, and Cole came in from left field. Ethan took off his mask and held it up. "I'm fine."

Mario placed his hand on Ethan's shoulder. "Son, you really need to focus on the ball, not on Paige's rear end. You don't need another concussion."

His teammates, who'd gathered around him, were laughing so hard they were bent over. *Great.*

Paige reached out a hand to help him up. He pulled her to him and kissed her in front of everyone. "Okay, I'm good," he announced to the spectators. The crowd went crazy. Cheers and whistles sounded over the clapping.

Paige looked stunned, but she had a smile on her face. Ethan replaced his mask and got into position.

"Ummm, Paige—could you stop wiggling your butt so I can concentrate?"

"Sorry. No can do."

Mario replaced his mask and yelled, "Play ball!"

Crack. Paige hit a line drive down the third-base line, past Roman's outstretched glove, and took off toward first. Cole ran forward to grab the ball and threw it to Chloe at second. Paige was safe at first base, and Ethan cheered. Roman shook his head. Ethan had never cheered for the opposing team before, but he couldn't help himself. He'd always cheer for Paige.

Ethan's team won, not that anyone was really keeping score. After the game Ethan signed balls, gloves, and shirts. He had never had so much fun. He posed for pictures with Nikki and Nora's team and with each girl separately.

He looked around for Paige, and finally spotted her chatting with a man in a suit and tie. He made his way over. Chloe had reached Paige before him, and he heard Chloe say, "Most people around here don't show up to a softball game in a tie."

Ethan thrust his hand out to the man. "Hi, I'm Ethan Reynolds."

"Allen Campbell. Paige's fiancé."

Paige turned on Allen. "We are not, nor were we ever engaged, Allen." Paige couldn't believe he had shown up. She shouldn't have put a note on the bookstore door announcing they were closed for the softball game.

"Let me take you out for a late lunch. I need to be in St. Paul for a signing."

People gathered around with phones in their hands. She could hear the whispers: "Is that Allen Campbell? The mystery writer?" Paige grabbed his wrist and led him away from her friends and the crowd of spectators. How dare he show up? She thought she'd been clear when she said no to his proposal. Seriously, who would propose to someone after being caught with another woman only days before? And Allen wondered why she turned him down?

When they were out of earshot, she turned on him. "What are you doing here, Allen?"

"Come on, Paige. Give us another chance."

"I gave you a chance after I saw you kissing one of my colleagues. Weeks later, I found you in the arms of another devoted fan. Or don't you remember?"

"Be reasonable. We're good together. Besides, she meant nothing to me. You took the entire scene out of context."

"Really? That's what you're going with?" She didn't know why she was having this conversation. They weren't good together; Allen just needed someone on his arm at dinner parties and to show his fans he was a loving and devoted partner instead of the playboy he really was. "I'm not sure how anyone could misinterpret a naked bimbo straddling you."

Had she seriously just seen a smirk on his face? Paige clenched her fists and pointed at the parking lot. "Get out of my sight." Allen had no right to show up in her town. All she needed was the locals comparing her to her mother.

"You heard the lady. It's time to leave, son."

Paige hadn't heard Abe come up behind her, and she turned to see Ethan and Chloe two steps behind him. The rest of the team gathered around her.

Allen backed up a few steps. "We're not over, Paige."

Ethan put his arm around her as she replied, "Yes Allen, we are."

Roman spoke up. "Let me show you the way to your car."

She loved her family and friends. Paige was so grateful for the united front they showed.

Ethan kissed her temple. "Forget about him. If you want to talk about it later, I'll be happy to listen. But right now, we have the town barbeque to get to. Let's not waste one more minute on that jerk."

Abe reached for her hand. "He's right, sweet pea. Let's eat."

CHAPTER SIXTEEN

*T*he next day, Paige tore through her closet trying to find something to wear for her date with Ethan. Chloe sat on the bed and watched her pull out dress after dress.

Paige held up a red satin number. "How about this one?"

"Nuh-uh. Hand it over." Chloe held out her hand. "That needs to go to the thrift store. Besides, if you can still fit into that, I'm going to off myself right now."

"This one?" Paige had brought the yellow polka-dot dress with her on a visit to her grandpa two years earlier.

Chloe wrinkled her nose. "What possessed you to buy that?"

"The lady at Saks told me polka dots were all the rage and it looked great on me."

An unladylike snort came from her best friend, and Paige flung the offending material onto the bed.

"Why didn't you bring anything nice to wear? I'm sure you have a gazillion dresses back in New York."

"I hadn't planned on dating."

"Where is Ethan taking you?"

"If I knew, I wouldn't be having this much trouble choosing

an outfit." Paige had just removed the fourth dress she'd tried on when the doorbell rang. "Shoot. Can you run down and answer?"

Chloe jumped off the bed. "I'm on it." She rushed down the stairs yelling, "I've got it," so Abe wouldn't have to move from his chair.

Chloe returned with a garment bag in her hand and a huge smile on her face.

"What's that? Who was at the door?"

"A delivery guy. There's a note." Chloe handed her an envelope.

Paige read the note aloud: "Maggie called me an idiot for not telling you where I was taking you tonight. She said you'd be worried about what to wear. It may be a little presumptuous of me, but I thought I'd take the guesswork out of the equation. Maggie approved. Hope you do, too. Ethan."

Paige covered her mouth with her hand. She was about to burst.

Chloe unzipped the bag and held up the sleeveless black dress for Paige.

"Did you know about this? Is this from your shop?"

"*May-be*."

"This whole time, you knew the dress was being delivered and you made me go through my closet?"

"Since we needed to kill time, I figured we'd purge your closet of ugly." Chloe smirked.

No guy had ever bought Paige clothing before. The short black dress was simple and casual with a flared hemline—the perfect dress to dance in. And she had the perfect heels to match.

"What are you waiting for? Try it on."

With a sway of her hips, she modeled the dress for Chloe. "What do you think?"

Chloe reached into her backpack and pulled out a pear-cut

onyx necklace with an antique silver-leaf wrap. "Here, turn around. I made it specifically for you."

Paige put on the matching earrings then hugged Chloe. "Thank you, they're beautiful."

"Don't you dare cry; you'll ruin your makeup."

AN HOUR LATER, Paige and Ethan arrived in Duluth and enjoyed a fabulous dinner at a Greek restaurant, then walked the path along the shore of Lake Superior in the direction of the dance club. Seagulls squawked and a long-short-short horn sounded. They stopped to watch a bulk carrier pass under the lift bridge. Paige pulled her wrap closed against the cool breeze coming off the lake. "I'm bummed I'll miss the tall ships coming in. I've missed it every year since the festival started."

Ethan took her hand in his. "Maybe you can come back for it?"

"Maybe, but I doubt my boss will allow another vacation so soon after I return."

They walked hand in hand until they reached the club. The club wasn't like one she'd ever attended. The old theatre-turned-nightclub was both elegant and romantic. Vintage Hollywood movie posters hung on the exposed brick walls, contrasting with the wood-and-metal railings and oversized chandeliers. Half-moon couches in deep emerald velvet flanked the stage, where a live band played music you could dance to—not like the clubs for twenty-somethings Paige had been to in her college days.

They danced for hours, lost in the music, lost in each other's touch as they moved together as one. Ethan held her low on her hips. His hands trailed down her back and pulled her close. His lips brushed her ear as he whispered, "Are you having fun?"

"I am," she whispered back as she nipped at his ear.

Ethan's hands sensually roamed over her body, bringing her in close enough to feel his growing erection. Paige felt playful but knew if she didn't stop soon there was no telling what would happen. She cleared her throat, wondering if she would be able to speak. "Let's get a drink," she suggested, her voice breathy.

Ethan led her off the dance floor and out the side door to a brick patio overlooking the lake. They stood at the railing. He placed her in front of him and wrapped his arms around her. "You're killin' me, Smalls."

Paige tilted her head back, her forehead against his cheek, and smiled. "I should have known you'd reference *The Sandlot*."

"One of my favorite movies." Ethan nuzzled her neck. His breath was hot, creating shivers down her spine. He kissed her temple. "I'll get us a drink. Don't go anywhere."

Paige watched as Ethan stepped up to the patio bar and ordered their drinks. She realized right then that Ethan Reynolds was her "one." Her grandma had told her that she'd know when the right one came along. There would be no denying the chemistry. And Paige couldn't deny it; she was falling in love with Ethan Reynolds.

"Here you go. Vodka lemonade."

Paige sipped the straw in a seductive way. At least, she hoped he was cluing in to what she had in mind. She never was good at flirting. She could write a flirty scene, but acting it out was something totally different.

Ethan set his glass on the railing and ran his hand over her arms and down her back, keeping her close. Being in Ethan's arms was intoxicating. They watched the iron ore ships in the distance. She could get drunk on his touch alone, no need for alcohol.

Paige was on fire and was ready to continue their dance elsewhere. Ethan made her feel sexy and confident. She didn't want the night to end and hoped to wake up in his arms come morning. "I'm ready to go if you are."

Ethan took her hand. "I was hoping you'd say that. Let's get out of here."

She'd never heard his voice drop so many octaves.

WHY HAD he decided to walk to the club? And why did he decide to take her to Duluth, a forty-five-minute drive, when all he could think of was removing each piece of her clothing slowly, ravishing her body. Maybe they should rent a hotel room for the night. No. Paige had responsibilities and needed to be close to home.

On their walk back to the car, Paige said, "We have a long drive. Let's play this or that."

"I don't think I've played that before." He'd play along, because he knew she was as energized as he was and needed to concentrate on something else.

Paige squeezed his hand. "It's easy, you'll catch on. Fall or winter?"

"Fall. Nothing beats the comfort food."

"Okay, then pumpkin or apple pie?"

Ethan had to think on that one. "Apple." He pulled her closer, his arm wrapped around her waist. "How about you?"

"Definitely fall, but pumpkin pie with lots of whipped cream." Paige licked her lips.

The mention of whipped cream had him hot and bothered in seconds. Except Cole came to mind. *What the hell?* It was the conversation he had with Cole earlier. It must have been the apple pie. Big Apple. New York. *Crap!* He'd been thinking of asking her a question. Something that gnawed at him. *I guess this is as good a time as any.*

"Paige? Can I ask you a question?"

"Sure." She laid her head on his shoulder as they approached the car.

"This probably isn't the best time to bring this up, but before we go any further, I've been wondering why you and Allen broke things off."

Paige stepped away from him, leaned against the car, and crossed her arms. This was a real mood changer, but she'd answer his questions. "Well, he was charming at first and I guess I was a little starstruck. I mean, a well-known mystery writer. He brought me to all the hip parties—all the ones I'd never have been invited to—and the parties proved to be helpful with schmoozing for donors." Paige shrugged. "After a few of the parties, I realized Allen enjoyed the attention he got with me on his arm. It seemed fame attracted the wrong women to him, and he liked it. You know, the type that find the challenge of a taken man more attractive."

Ethan nodded. "Unfortunately, yes."

Paige continued, "When I found him in bed with another woman, I broke it off immediately."

Ethan hugged her close. "I'm sorry. I shouldn't have brought it up."

"I'm glad you asked."

Ethan opened the door for Paige, and she slid into the buttery leather seat. He walked around to the other side. Ethan retreated into his thoughts, stuck on the word Paige had used: *starstruck*. The smile he'd worn all night was hard to maintain. He didn't much feel like smiling anymore. *Is this the reason Paige wants to be with me? Would being with me add to the popularity of her charity?* He wasn't even playing baseball anymore.

Paige placed her hand over his. "Are you okay?"

With a half-smile he glanced at her. "Yeah. Of course."

With his mind reeling, the game resumed, but Ethan only gave the one-word answers, not elaborating or asking any more questions of his own. Mentally rehashing his last conversation with Cole, when he'd warned him about a long-distance relationship with someone who didn't visit Minnesota very often, had him pulling away from the beautiful, caring woman sitting next to him. His heart was at stake once again, and he wouldn't let it break into a million pieces. He'd built a home in Deer Creek Falls to be closer to his family. Could he give it up and take the chance on love?

Almost home, he realized Paige had gone quiet. Ethan had ruined their perfect evening by bringing up her ex, which in turn brought up his insecurities. He wanted to bang his head against the steering wheel. At least he'd found out why she went out with the famous mystery writer before things progressed to the bedroom.

Ethan pulled into Paige's driveway and she looked to him, confused.

He was an idiot. He could be making Paige breakfast in the morning, and instead he was dropping her off at home.

He parked in front of Abe's house and reached for Paige's hand. "Let me walk you in."

"No need." Paige opened the door and hurried out.

Ethan rolled down the window. "Paige."

"I had a nice night, thank you," she answered, then walked into the house, never looking back.

WHAT THE HELL HAPPENED? Paige wondered. She watched from behind the curtain of the living-room window as Ethan drove away. She knew he wanted her as much as she wanted him. Something had changed after she answered his question about

Allen, but she didn't know what. She texted Chloe on her way up the stairs to her bedroom.

I'm home.

How did it go?

Hot then cold.

Thirty minutes later, Paige held her glass out to Chloe to fill. Chloe had shown up with a bottle of wine and a pint of Ben and Jerry's for each of them—Half Baked for Paige, and Strawberry Cheesecake for herself. She had a knack for knowing the right time for a pity party.

Chloe passed Paige a spoon. "Tell me what happened. And start from the beginning."

She told Chloe about the dance club and the best Greek food she'd ever eaten. "After dinner, we danced. It was a scene right out of frickin' *Dirty Dancing*." Paige waved her spoon around wildly. "We left in a rush before we combusted on the dance floor, but then he just dropped me off at home. No explanation!" Paige gouged out another spoonful of ice cream, shoved it into her mouth, and collapsed on the bed.

"I really thought by the way he ushered me off the dance floor we'd be continuing the dance at his house."

Chloe held up her spoon and fanned herself. "And then he dropped you off? I'm confused. What happened between the club and here?"

Paige groaned. "I don't know. Like I said, hot then cold."

"Sounds like he got cold feet."

"Do men get cold feet? Isn't sex all they think about?"

"Probably and yes." Chloe rolled her eyes.

"Okay, enough about me," Paige said. "Tell me about your love life."

"Sorry, no can do. I'm living vicariously through you."

They were both lying on the bed, looking up at the ceiling. At the same time, they sighed and said, "We're pathetic."

Chloe looked at Paige. "Ethan loves you, I'm sure of it. Give him time to work through things and you'll see, it'll be worth it."

Paige yawned. They'd polished off the bottle and their pints of ice cream. "Do you think Ethan will still want to go to the gala with me?"

Chloe got up, grabbed the empty containers, and dumped them in the garbage can by Paige's desk. "I don't know, but hopefully he'll come to his senses and realize what he has right in front of him. I'm heading home. Call me if you need anything."

"Thanks, Chloe." After her friend left, Paige curled up, hugged her pillow, and fell asleep.

CHAPTER SEVENTEEN

*T*he early morning roll of thunder and light rainfall had brought out the aroma of fresh-cut grass and summer flowers. Paige watched as a robin pulled a worm from the damp soil as she returned from her run. This morning she felt like the worm. Pulled out of her comfort zone as she contemplated what came next. The sun shone brightly now, and the humidity hung in the air. A feeling of dread rose to the surface as she showered and gathered her things. She headed to town to open the bookstore. Paige couldn't get Ethan out of her mind. She kept checking her phone, hoping he'd call. She didn't know what she'd done wrong. Maybe he was having second thoughts about pursuing a relationship. The days she'd spent with him planning the festival and getting to know him better had been idyllic. It wasn't his celebrity or that he'd bought the building to help her grandfather settle a debt—it was Ethan. They had fun together, they laughed, and she thought he genuinely cared for her. She sipped her coffee, swallowing against the lump in her throat.

Paige gathered some chalk and decorated the sidewalk chalkboard sign. She drew an arrow pointing toward the store and captioned it, "This way . . . BOOKS." Then, she drew an arrow pointing in the opposite direction and wrote, "That way? Bears maybe? We wouldn't risk it." After hauling it onto the sidewalk, she stood back and admired her handiwork. Hopefully the sign would attract some much-needed customers.

A woman with beautiful olive skin, high cheekbones, and long black hair pulled back into a loose bun approached Paige carrying a basket. "Good morning!" She laughed. "I love your sign."

"Thank you." Paige moved the sign into position.

"My name is Lily, and these are for you." Lily held out the basket to Paige. "They're from Rosie. She heard about your breakup. I'm sorry."

Paige groaned and opened the linen cloth, uncovering peach streusel muffins. She didn't think she and Ethan had broken up. "Okay. Well, this is awkward."

"Tell me about it," Lily said. "I'm still getting used to small-town life."

"If you have time, come on in and have one. I just brewed a pot of coffee." They walked into the bookstore. "Are you new to town?" Paige set the basket on the front counter.

Lily walked to the self-serve coffee station. "Do you take it black?"

"Yes. Thank you, but I should be serving you coffee."

Lily waved her off. "Nonsense. I'm used to serving others. And yes, to answer your question, I just moved to town last month and am working a few shifts at the café."

"Please, have a seat." Paige motioned to a pair of wingback chairs. "I take it you're from a big city."

Lily set the cups down on the small table between the two chairs. "I am. I grew up in Pittsburgh but moved here from New York City."

"That's where I live. I grew up here, and I'm only back for a little while to help my grandpa out with the store." They talked as they ate, and she learned Lily had worked for Saks Fifth Avenue designing window displays. They discovered they'd frequented some of the same restaurants and commiserated about not having a coffee shop in town.

"I love your store. I understand this is a temporary space."

"It is." As if on cue, the whine of a saw and the screech of a drill pierced the air from next door.

Per Abe's request, she wouldn't mention the possibility of the store closing. She worried her grandpa still held out hope that she would move home, but for her to consider moving home she would need to reconstruct her life. The thought kept her up at night. The song "Should I Stay or Should I Go" by the Clash had played in her head like a broken record since Ethan dropped her off the night before.

"I actually came in to find a book on crocheting. I used to belong to a crochet and knitting group at church to relieve stress. They jokingly referred to themselves as the Hookers."

Paige laughed. "Sounds like a fun group."

"It was. I asked Rosie if she knew of a group here in town, and she didn't, but suggested I start one. Rosie mentioned you may have a space available where we could meet." Lily hurried on, "I could definitely pay."

"Don't be silly." Although Paige was reluctant to offer a space for the few months she knew they would remain open, it would bring in foot traffic. "You're welcome to meet here anytime."

Lily glanced around the store. "I have an idea. Let me go grab something."

Paige watched as an enthusiastic Lily hurried from the store. "I'll be right back," she called, halfway out the door. The way Lily bounced from the store made Paige think of Tigger from the Winnie the Pooh stories.

Fifteen minutes later, with a large canvas tote in hand and slightly out of breath, Lily walked through the door. "Sorry it took me so long."

Paige chuckled. Lily was a breath of fresh air. She had gathered several books in anticipation of Lily's return and placed them on the table.

"These are great!" Lily exclaimed.

Paige watched the whirlwind happening before her. Lily unpacked a bright, multicolored floral granny-square blanket from her bag, scrunched and draped it over the table, arranged the books around it, and stood back.

"What do you think? If you had other items from local artists, I could display them throughout the store with corresponding books."

"This is fantastic!" Paige said. Lily's enthusiasm was starting to rub off on her.

"I enjoy making stores come alive."

"Maybe I should join your group and learn to crochet to relieve stress. Do you accept beginners into your club?"

"I'd be happy to teach you! Would you mind if I used the chalkboard sign to advertise the new group?"

"Not at all. I'm running out of ideas for clever ways to get people into the store."

Before Lily left, they decided on a day and time when she would come by to decorate the sign. Lily's extroversion left Paige's introverted head spinning, but now with the bookstore so quiet, her thoughts were in danger of returning to Ethan.

To keep her mind occupied, she pulled books and rearranged the DIY section.

Paige glanced at her watch as Chloe strolled in.

"Just finished the jewelry set for the silent auction," Chloe said with a smile on her face. She pulled a small black box out of a bag and set it on the front counter. "And I brought lunch."

Paige opened the black leather box lined with black satin. The necklace featured four rings of hammered sterling silver with three freshwater pearls and a beautiful offset multicolored glass gem. The earrings mirrored the necklace. "Chloe, this is gorgeous! Are you sure you want to give it away?"

Chloe shrugged. "It's a great cause. Why wouldn't I?"

"Well, thank you. I hope you included business cards."

"They're in the bag. Let's eat." Chloe didn't take compliments well, but Paige could tell she was pleased by her reaction.

"Great, I'm starving. How did you get away from the store? It looked like you were busy."

"My mom stopped by." Chloe pulled sandwiches from a paper sack. "She's the one who made these; she figured you were all alone and wouldn't have brought anything with you. She's watching the store until I get back."

Paige hugged Chloe. "I'll be sure to thank your mom." She was overwhelmed by the generosity and support from her friends and the community. Paige didn't know how she was going to leave and not feel a huge sense of loss. In years past when she'd visited her grandpa, she never had a problem leaving, but being in Deer Creek Falls for more than a month had her seriously reevaluating her life choices.

Chloe nodded toward the front table where Lily had arranged her artwork. "Nice display. I didn't think you crocheted."

"I don't," Paige said. "Have you met Lily? She's new to town and works part-time at the café."

"Yeah, very energetic—that's Lily's work?" Chloe took a bite of her roast-beef-and-cheddar croissant sandwich.

Paige nodded. "Yes, she was in this morning." She told Chloe about their conversation and shared her frustration at how the only other customer who'd come into the store wanted to know where the souvenir shop had gone. "Lily offered to create a display for different artisans."

"Sounds like she's onto something."

Florals by Fran was Ethan's next stop. He pulled to the curb, got out of his truck with a paper bag in hand, and approached Fran's signature bright-pink door and lime-green awning. He reached for the brass knob and stepped inside. The intoxicating fragrance of roses and peonies greeted him like a warm blanket. Ethan hadn't called ahead, and he probably should have, since several customers were browsing the cases.

"Ethan!" Fran's friendly voice carried over the store. "I bet I know what you're here for."

That damn Town Talk app. He guessed he had it coming. Fran came around the corner, and he hugged the petite woman. Her gray curls tickled his chin. She backed up and adjusted her multi-colored reading glasses. "Honey, you keep getting better looking with age." She swatted him. "Come on, let's see what you have in mind for a make-up bouquet."

The deep baritone voice of the town's only lawyer asked, "Fran, how do you always know what people are shopping for?"

"Oh, please. After forty years in this town, I know when things go amiss. You are always here on Fridays because you put in too many long hours and want to treat your lovely wife to her favorite flowers." She placed a gentle hand on his arm. "She's a lucky woman to have such a caring and devoted man. I'll have the roses and peonies delivered to your house before three this afternoon."

He bent over and kissed her cheek. "Thanks, Fran." He nodded to Ethan. "Nice to see you, son. Good luck."

Fran turned to Ethan. "Now. You're going to need a bouquet for Paige. I'm guessing you had a misunderstanding. Show me what you have in that bag of yours."

Ethan opened the bag and slid out six yellow number-two pencils and a mini-notebook with a cat on the cover. "What can you do with these in a bouquet?"

Fran clapped her hands. "Oh, this is fun!" She turned and

retrieved a vase off the shelf behind her and held up her hand, telling him to wait a minute. She rushed into the back and came out with a few yellow roses and some white daisies.

"Now tell me. Friends or lovers?"

"Um . . . well."

"Ha! I knew it." She replaced the yellow roses with pink-tipped white ones, and added pink peonies, lavender, magenta gerbera daisies, and a few stems of greenery. She twisted floral wire around a pencil. "Something like this?"

"You're amazing."

"Well hon, I'm not done yet. Come back in an hour and I'll have something special waiting. Paige will love it." She slid the notebook to him. "Write something romantic on the first page. It can be the card."

She handed him a pen but he hesitated, watching her as she selected more flowers from the cooler.

"Don't worry," she assured him. "I might read the notes, but I never tell anyone."

THE BELL chimed at the bookstore, and in walked Ethan with a large, gorgeous bouquet of flowers.

Chloe stood. "That's my cue to leave." She lowered her voice. "Call me later." She walked by Ethan on her way out and said, "Go get 'er, tiger."

"Bye, Chloe."

He lowered the bouquet and crinkled his brow at Paige. "Forgive me?"

"It's fine."

"It's not fine. I should have explained. I led you to believe we were going back to my house." He moved closer and placed the bouquet on the counter.

"The flowers are stunning. Thank you." Paige breathed in the scent of lavender and roses and opened the cover of the notebook to read Ethan's note: *When you smile, it lights up a room and when you kiss me, my heart skips a beat. Please forgive me.*

It was hard to stay mad at Ethan, even though she was still confused by his behavior.

Ethan moved around the counter, turned her to face him, and placed a hand on her cheek, tracing his thumb over her bottom lip.

"Ethan, I understand. I'm returning to New York and you live here. It's not fair to ask you to start a relationship when we live so far apart."

"You're right. Being far apart scares me and was the reason for my cowardly retreat last night. I don't want to screw this up and I don't want what's happening between us to end. I want us to be together, but I know how much you love New York and your job. I'm willing to make a long-distance relationship work if you're willing to give it a chance."

"I'd like that." As she spoke, Ethan's eyes were on her mouth.

He leaned forward and brushed his lips against hers questioningly, and she answered by deepening the kiss.

Feeling light-headed, she pulled back and looked over his shoulder. "We have an audience."

"Good, let them gawk." He leaned into the embrace once more.

She pushed him away slightly and hid behind him.

Ethan looked over his shoulder toward the picture window and waved to the intruder. "Yep. Aunt Emma must have spotted me entering the store with the flowers."

"Who else is out there?" Paige asked, not wanting to look.

"Who cares? Now, where were we?"

CHAPTER EIGHTEEN

his was how Cinderella must have felt. Paige stepped out of the black limo Ethan had arranged for the night and intertwined her arm in his. Cameras flashed, and there was a buzz in the air as people watched from beyond the roped-off area that led into the ballroom. Henry and Michael had really outdone themselves by arranging for the press coverage.

She and Henry had started Project Night-Light five years earlier, and every year they had to book a larger venue. Their goal was for their charity to become a national organization. The previous year, they'd expanded twofold and known they couldn't plan the event with volunteers any longer. Michael, Henry's partner, had risen to the challenge.

"This is amazing. A children's fairy tale come to life," Paige said.

Ethan squeezed her hand. "I couldn't agree more."

The ceiling glistened with twinkle lights and the music, a quirky and whimsical instrumental melody, created an atmosphere of frolic. She envisioned toys in a toy chest coming to life. Faux candlelight adorned high-top round tables with white linen tablecloths, and the room shimmered with the effect of fireflies dancing in the night sky.

Ethan picked up a place card from one of the tables and read it aloud. "'And I can do 'most anything if I only think I can.' Nice touch, using quotes from children's books," he said.

She swallowed hard. What were the chances Ethan would pick up the first one and it would be from his favorite children's story?

Henry strode toward them. He looked dapper in his tuxedo and Dr. Seuss bow tie. She couldn't help but smile. Only Henry could pull off that look in a room full of high-society donors.

Henry took both her hands in his and held her arms out to get a good look at her. He whistled. "You're gorgeous."

Paige blushed like she always did when he complimented her, but secretly loved it. "Thank you."

Ethan cleared his throat and stepped forward. "Hi, I'm Ethan Reynolds." He held out a hand to Henry.

Henry's mouth opened and closed, and he reached out to shake Ethan's hand. "Now I know who's been occupying Paige's time." He winked at her.

A waiter came by with a tray of champagne flutes. Ethan took two off the tray and handed one to Paige.

Henry also took one and raised his glass. "Here's to our biggest turnout yet."

Paige clinked her glass against Henry's. "I'm ecstatic. If I could do it in these heels, I'd be jumping up and down and cheering. Let's hope everyone came with deep pockets so we reach our goal."

They'd received inquiries from all over the country about bringing Project Night-Light to other cities. The idea of further expansion was both exciting and nerve-racking at the same time.

Michael approached their small group with a woman on his arm. He looked stunning in his tuxedo with his short, wavy black hair and piercing blue eyes. Henry was a lucky man. Michael kissed Paige on the cheek. "Good evening, beautiful. What do you think?"

"You've done a fantastic job recreating our vision. It's breathtaking."

"Thank you, I had fun." Michael turned slightly to the dark-haired beauty. "Paige, I'd like to introduce you to my cousin Kate Davis. She's here visiting me from Chicago."

Paige held out her hand. "It's so nice to meet you, Kate. Are you the renowned pastry-chef cousin I hear so much about?"

"I don't know about renowned." Kate swatted at Michael's shoulder. "But yes, I'm his cousin and a pastry chef."

Michael glanced at Ethan. "Now, who is this?"

"I'm sorry. Michael, this is Ethan Reynolds, my date tonight."

Michael and Ethan shook hands. "It's about time I finally get to meet the man I've read so much about."

"Hopefully those days are over," Ethan said.

Michael looked confused at Ethan's comment. Paige stared meaningfully at Henry, who cleared his throat and said, "Michael, Kate, I see the Daningers. I'd love for you to meet them."

"It was nice to meet you both," Kate said, and Michael concurred. "Please excuse us." Michael, Kate, and Henry walked off to schmooze with the couple, who were amongst the charity's biggest donors.

Paige and Ethan moved around the room greeting guests as they made their way toward the silent-auction items. Ethan stayed close, making her feel special. Never in a million years had she thought she'd be here with him.

Ethan was a natural in his ability to work a room. His body of knowledge ranged from sports to politics and everything in between.

Over the last month, she had gotten to know the real Ethan, rather than the man who'd filled the pages of her book—his caring and generosity toward others, his friendly and easygoing nature, and the way he always made her laugh. She had fallen in love with him.

When they reached the silent-auction area, Paige listened to the whispered conversations. "Exquisite craftsmanship," "one of a kind," and "fabulous" were a few of the terms used to describe the items.

She glanced at the slip of paper next to Chloe's jewelry set and couldn't believe the triple-digit figure in front of her. Next to her, a woman snapped a picture of the walnut entryway table Cole had donated. The natural live-edge table was covered with resin to look like ocean waves washing up on a shore. The woman turned to her friend and mentioned how they needed to contact the artist for a feature article in the next edition of their magazine. Paige whispered in Ethan's ear, "Did you hear that?"

"Yeah, good for him. He creates beautiful pieces; it's about time someone noticed."

Even the bright and whimsical crocheted blanket Lily donated had reached a bid of over one thousand dollars, and the night was still young.

Henry lightly tapped Ethan on the shoulder. "May I steal Paige away for a few minutes? There are a few donors we need to make nice with. Besides, I believe part of your fan base is at a table behind you," he said.

"Sure, I'll try to get some donors for you."

Ethan squeezed Paige's hand and whispered in her ear, "Save me a dance." He kissed her cheek and nodded to Henry.

Paige nodded at the appropriate times and made small talk with the couple Henry introduced her to. When the couple moved on, Henry said, "Paige, I see a friend. I'll be right back."

He waved to the small group as he made his way toward them. Paige adored Henry. His charisma had donors reaching into their pockets and handing him checks. He laughed and joked with the crowd around him as if it came naturally to him.

Outgoing and charismatic, she was not. Paige had a job to do and she would do her best, but as she made her way around the room, she realized this wasn't her life anymore. Paige didn't feel grounded like she did when she was in her hometown. She enjoyed the down-to-earth people she grew up with.

Henry was back, waving a hand in front of her face. "Earth to Paige."

Paige smiled. "Sorry, I blanked. You know how exhausted I get faking extroversion."

"Yes. I do. But listen, Margo just walked in and is talking with Ethan." Henry nodded toward the center of the room.

Paige grabbed Henry's forearm. "Does she know I'm dating Ethan?"

Hopefully Margo wouldn't put two and two together. If Margo realized she was dating a baseball player, she might reveal her secret. Not good.

"I didn't even know you were bringing him, much less dating him. Which by the way, you could have told me!"

"Really? You're reprimanding me now, when my life is in the balance? What if Margo tells him before I can? He'll never speak to me again."

"Stop being so dramatic. He's obviously smitten, the way he keeps stealing glances at you." Henry's voice dropped to a whisper. "Michael almost outed you, and would have if I hadn't seen the Daningers. I'll go and distract them and save your bacon. But you need to tell him soon. Give me a few minutes, then make your way toward us."

Paige bit down on her lip. How had this become so complicated? She had turned off her heart because of her mother's history with men, and knew she had never genuinely loved any of the guys she dated until now.

Would Ethan hate her when he found out that he was her inspiration?

ETHAN COULDN'T HELP STEALING glances at Paige as he made small talk with fans. He'd catch her glancing at him, too. He was enjoying himself but couldn't wait for the gala to end. He wanted Paige all to himself.

A woman approached him. She introduced herself as Margo, an editor for Cagney & Cahill. "I recognize you, you're Ethan Reynolds."

"I am. You must know Paige Turner?"

"I do. How do you know Paige?"

"We grew up in the same town."

"You must be her muse!"

"Margo! Thank you for coming," Henry said, swooping in.

Ethan didn't have time to question Margo thanks to Henry's interruption, but now he knew for sure. The woman he'd fallen in love with had written a book about him. Wow.

"Excuse me. Could I get your autograph?"

Ethan turned around and smiled at a group of young women. "Of course." He signed their programs.

Ethan caught Paige's eye across the room and smiled as she walked toward him.

PAIGE HAD NEVER FELT MORE attractive than she did with Ethan. Allen had never made her feel beautiful. His ego got in the way, always promoting himself and flirting with his female fans.

No matter if Ethan was signing autographs or conversing with guests, his gaze always came back to her. Ethan made her pulse race. He made her feel important.

The energy in the room sizzled like a live wire. It was time for her to give her speech and encourage people to donate to Project Night-Light.

Henry approached her and asked, "Are you ready?"

She was. Paige took several deep breaths as Henry guided her to the stage. She hated being in the public eye, so she focused on her debate-team days and gathered her courage. Paige felt strong —more energized and more confident with Ethan there.

She stepped up to the microphone. "Good evening. My name is Paige Turner. I'm one of the founders of Project Night-Light. Thank you all for coming tonight. I hope you are enjoying your-selves." The audience clapped.

"My grandfather, one of the wittiest and most well-read men I know, owns an independent bookstore in my small hometown in northern Minnesota. So to say books have always been a part of my life is quite the understatement." Some audience members nodded, some chuckled.

"My mother was eighteen when she gave birth to me. Her dreams didn't include a child, and when I was four years old, she left me to be raised by my grandparents. They were wonderful, and I knew I was loved every hour of every day, but I struggled with aban-donment issues over the years and turned to books as an escape.

"Books transported me to distant lands where magic beanstalks reached into the heavens, fairy godmothers turned pumpkins into enchanted coaches, and trains chugged up moun-tains reminding us we shouldn't give up, no matter how much we wanted to."

Paige looked up to see Ethan nodding.

"During my freshman year of college, I volunteered at an elementary school. Mostly I worked with students who struggled with reading and math, but when it was library day, I'd walk the students to the library and help them find a book to take home. After the children checked out their books, we'd gather in a cozy corner of the library and I would read to them.

"One day, a little boy I'd been working with on his reading skills told me he wished he could take more than one book home. I told the teacher what he'd said and asked if he could possibly check out a few more books. This little boy lived in a shelter and had very few possessions.

"I remember thinking how very lucky I was to have grown up surrounded by books, with a roof over my head, and never having to worry about where my next meal would come from. I knew I had to do something to get books into the hands of children who needed them as an escape from their realities, and started Project Night-Light.

"I gathered a group of friends, one of whom was my dear friend Henry Brandt"—Paige looked to Henry and winked—"and we raised enough money to buy a small bookshelf filled with books for the local shelter. It didn't stop there, though. People heard what we were doing, and pretty soon we had to rent a storage locker to keep all the books that were donated.

"Today, any child in need receives a blanket, a night-light, a pair of pajamas, and a tote bag full of books." Paige scanned the audience, purposely pausing at the donors in front of her. "It's because of all of you that Project Night-Light serves underprivileged children in five states and has hit number four on the top-ten list of literary charities in the country. With your help tonight, we are hoping to expand into two more states this year." Applause erupted.

"Thank you." Henry stood next to her and clapped. When the applause subsided, she said, "I also want to thank Henry's amazing partner, Michael Davis from Splendid Soirées, for organizing this event, along with all the volunteers who work hard to make children's dreams come true."

She handed the microphone to Henry, who reminded everyone the silent auction would end at ten p.m., thanked them for their generous donations, introduced the band, and encouraged everyone to have fun and dance.

Paige was surrounded by donors and had already tried to excuse herself several times when Ethan stepped forward. "Excuse me, could I have this dance?" She heard the women whisper as Ethan led her to the dance floor.

Ethan pulled her close and whispered, "I've been waiting all night for this moment."

Their lips met and her body tingled. She loved how they fit together. In his arms was her new favorite place. The band played, "All I Want Is You" by U2 as they held each other.

"I love this song," Paige said as she ran her fingers through his hair and gazed into his eyes.

Ethan placed a kiss on her temple. "Me too. I think we have our song."

"I think we do."

He kissed her again, the song ending too soon. The next song started: "What a Wonderful World."

They danced until the silent auction concluded and said their goodbyes to Henry and Michael.

PAIGE CUDDLED close to Ethan in the back of the limo and slipped her hand into his. "Ethan, I need to tell you something," she whispered.

He moved his hand to her side, then pulled her onto his lap. Several blonde strands had come loose from her updo, and her dress exposed her long, tanned legs. He couldn't resist running his hand along her leg.

Paige stopped his hand. "Please, let me say what I need to say before we get back to my apartment."

Ethan had an idea what she was about to tell him, and he needed to be patient. He wanted her naked but knew that couldn't happen in the back of the limo anyway. "Okay."

The nervous way she bit down on her lower lip made him want to ravish her mouth. He found it sexy and endearing at the same time.

"So, you read the book *Catch Me*?"

He might as well have a little fun. "I did. Can we recreate a few of the scenes?"

"Definitely, but after what I have to tell you, you may not want to."

He kissed her neck. "Doubtful." He decided to cut the conversation short. "Plus, I already know you're the author."

Breathless, she asked, "You do?"

"Uh-huh."

"And . . . what do you think of that?"

"I enjoyed the book, and I fell in love with the author—with you."

Paige stopped his hand from moving farther north, and he grinned like a fool. "You're not mad?" she asked.

"Not at all." He kissed her forehead and looked into her eyes. "If you want to call yourself L.C. Brooks, that's fine, and if you want to write about us, that's fine too. I'm happy to supply you with enough material for a million books."

"Wait. How long have you known?"

The limo pulled to the curb. "We're here, sir."

"Let's talk in the morning. Right now, all I want is you."

Ethan helped Paige off his lap and onto the sidewalk. A light rain drizzled down on them. He took her hand and they walked quickly through the door of her building when the doorman opened it for them.

Even though his home was now in Minnesota, he'd find a way to make their relationship work. Even if they had to split their time between DCF and NYC. He wasn't giving her up for anything.

They were finally alone as they stepped into the elevator. Paige placed a hand to his chest and looked into his eyes with such passion, he leaned her against the wall. Their tongues clashed as he massaged her nipple through her satin dress, bringing it to a peak.

The elevator settled and the doors opened behind him. Ethan broke the kiss and took Paige's hand. He turned right and heard Paige giggle.

"Wrong way, Romeo."

Ethan scooped her up in his arms and hurried in the opposite direction. "Which number?"

Paige sucked on his earlobe. "812," she breathed, simultaneously unbuttoning his shirt. He set her down. She opened her clutch and with shaky fingers unlocked the door. Ethan flung it open and scooped her up again, and they stumbled blindly into the entry as their tongues sparred once again.

He kicked the door shut behind him.

"Set me down," she said quietly.

He did as she asked, and she stepped back, reached behind her neck, and seductively undid a button. The silky dress slid down over her curves, and Paige stepped out of the pool of fabric that gathered around her feet.

She bit her lower lip and Ethan swallowed. This was his sexy-librarian fantasy come to life, and he couldn't look away as she stood before him in only her heels and a scrap of satin panties. He had never seen anyone more beautiful. He kicked off his shoes, ripped off his shirt, and moved close.

He wanted to slow down, to savor every minute. He cupped her face and placed a gentle kiss on her lips, then trailed kisses down her neck. She moaned and extended her neck to give him better access. As he sucked and nipped, he moved her smooth panties aside with his fingers. Ethan knew that this was going to be better than any love scene she could ever write.

PAIGE OPENED her eyes to the smell of coffee and gave a luxurious stretch.

Ethan walked through her bedroom door in his snug black boxer shorts, carrying two steaming mugs. "Good morning, beautiful."

She licked her lips and smiled.

He placed the mugs on the nightstand and crawled in next to her. "If you keep staring at me like that, your coffee will be cold before you get a chance to drink it."

With a polished fingernail, she traced a path down his chest and he emitted a low groan. She made her way lower, extending their morning playtime.

After they showered and dressed, Ethan packed his bag and set it by the front door. He had a flight to Boston to catch in a few hours, and Paige needed to meet with Margo before flying back to Minnesota.

"I really wish I hadn't made plans in Boston. Had I known we'd be taking our relationship to the next level, I would have postponed my trip. We could have spent the day in bed," Ethan said as he came up behind her and trailed a hand down her back.

Paige refilled their coffee mugs and spread peanut butter on toast. Two things she always had on hand were a loaf of bread in the freezer and a jar of peanut butter in the cupboard.

"I'm sorry I don't have much else to offer you for breakfast."

He wrapped his arms around her. "I already had breakfast." He trailed kisses down her neck and Paige's breathing quickened.

Paige turned around in his arms. "Well, Romeo, as much as I want to continue this, I'm starving. Besides, you need to tell me when you realized I was L.C. Brooks." She extracted herself and brought their meager breakfast to the table.

Ethan sat and pulled her onto his lap. "A lot of little things, I guess. My grandma insisting that I read a romance novel. The day we stopped by your grandma's bench and I realized her maiden name was Brooks. Then there was your ringtone. Of course, being called your muse solidified it even more."

"Why didn't you say something?"

He nuzzled her neck. "I wanted to see where this was going."

"And now?"

"Now I know a bit more about the life you have here in New York, and I'm determined we're going to make this long-distance relationship work."

"I'd love that."

Ethan kissed her fully on the lips and then sighed. "I'm really glad you caught me, but I have to catch my flight."

Paige laughed and stood. She walked him to the door and wrapped her arms around his neck, breakfast forgotten. "Say hi to Luke, and I'll see you in Minnesota."

After a scorching kiss, he walked out the door.

She traced her puffy lips with her finger. She could never have enough of the taste and feel of Ethan Reynolds.

CHAPTER NINETEEN

*P*aige sat in the conference room adjacent to Margo's office on Monday morning, not believing what she was hearing. "Let me get this straight. You want to buy the first three books in my series, sign a contract for exclusive rights for my next three books, and use Ethan's celebrity to promote *Catch Me*—a book I've already marketed and built a fan base for—after you turned me down once already?"

Paige was about to lose her shit. She clenched and unclenched her hands to keep from saying something she might regret. *Breathe, Paige.*

"Exactly." Margo smiled and nodded enthusiastically. "I should never have listened to Allen, and besides, in my defense, I didn't know you based your character on a Gold Glove winner and one of the most eligible bachelors in the sports world three years running. The fact you two went to high school together and are now dating adds up to the perfect marketing campaign." Margo slid the contract across the table to Paige.

She skimmed the contract. A month earlier, if Margo had made an offer, she might have signed her name. But not now. A month earlier, she thought she needed a large publishing house to pick up her book to be validated as a writer. A month earlier, she was still hiding her author identity from Allen because he thought independent authors weren't any good if they couldn't land a traditional deal. Except now she knew better. Her books were loved by many.

"Wait, back up. What do you mean you shouldn't have listened to Allen?"

By the look on Margo's face, it was clear she hadn't meant to mention Allen. "Oh . . . nothing. Never mind." Margo waved it off.

Paige had had enough. So, Allen knew she was L.C. Brooks? Was it possible he'd opened her laptop and gone through her files? Was talking with Margo a way for him to punish her for turning down his proposal? The time frame fit. She knew publishing could be a cutthroat business, but to use her relationship with Ethan to sell books? She'd never have thought it of Margo. Paige would never exploit Ethan.

She stood and slid the contract back to her boss. "I'm not interested."

Margo's smile disappeared. "What? I worked all night to put this offer together. What do you mean you're not interested?" Margo came out of her chair. "This is a good deal. You're not going to get another one like this!"

It was Paige's turn to smile. "I don't need Cagney and Cahill to be a successful author." She stopped herself from saying more. While Margo stared at her, speechless, Paige woke her phone, swiped, typed, and hit send. Margo's phone buzzed. "You have my resignation. I'll go pack my desk."

As she walked back to her cubicle, Paige received a text alert on her phone. Ethan.

I can't stop thinking of you. Heart emoji.

She texted back, *See you in a few days*. Smiley face with hearts emoji. She typed "love you," then deleted it and hit send.

Thirty minutes later, Paige made her way to the elevator holding a box of personal items. Henry followed silently until they reached the lobby.

"I'm going to miss you." Henry took the box from her and set it on the floor, then wrapped her in a hug. "You better come visit," he said.

"You know I will. Plus, we still have our charity. Besides, I followed your advice." Paige smiled through blurry eyes.

"What?!" Henry placed his hand over his heart. "I never!"

Henry, always so dramatic. She laughed. "Oh yes you did. You told me I didn't need Cagney and Cahill, that I needed to trust myself."

"Okay, that does sound like me."

Paige hugged him again. "I've got to go. I love you, Henry."

"Be still my heart," Henry said.

Paige picked up her box of items and walked away from the office building she'd loved coming to just a short time ago. She couldn't wait to get back to Minnesota, to Ethan, her grandpa, and all her friends. She had a bookstore to reinvent, and she knew just how to do it.

ETHAN DRESSED and followed the rich aroma coming from the kitchen.

"I wondered when you'd wake up." Luke filled a cup with coffee and handed it to him.

"Thanks. What did I do to deserve breakfast?"

Luke shrugged. "We need to eat." He slid a plate piled with scrambled eggs across the island. "Have you decided to accept the job?"

"I have, even though I was offered a coaching position at our old high school I would have loved. Paige lives and works in New York, so I accepted the position in the city."

"Wow, you've got it bad."

Ethan grinned. "I guess I do. Remember when Dad said that the minute he held Mom's hand, he knew she was the one?"

"Yeah, he was a romantic." Luke looked away.

Ethan understood how the mention of their father could hit him like a ton of bricks, and he had to fight off his own surge of emotion.

"It wasn't quite that fast, but she's definitely the one. I can't stop thinking about her."

Luke refilled his cup. "I'm happy for you."

Luke didn't seem himself. He was usually in much more of a hurry with the demands of running his own company. Something wasn't right. "Aren't you supposed to be at work?" Ethan asked.

Luke shrugged him off. "I told Grace I wouldn't be in. She's rearranging my schedule."

With a mouth full of eggs, Ethan stared at his brother. "What's going on? You don't take days off."

"Can't I spend time with my little brother? Speaking of which, I scored two tickets to tonight's home game. Are you interested?"

"Hell yes. I'm in."

CHAPTER TWENTY

*P*aige sat at a table at the back of Rosie's Café, talking with Chloe, Maggie, and Alexis. Although Chloe had been her best friend since grade school, the last few weeks had allowed them time to grow even closer.

Maggie and Alexis had welcomed her into their close-knit group with no hesitations, something she hadn't experienced with women she met in college. She hadn't realized how lonely she'd been until now.

Paige explained to Chloe that Ethan had already known she was L.C. Brooks.

"Ethan already knew?" Chloe asked.

Alexis turned away from her side conversation with Maggie. "We all knew," she said.

"Did you tell?" Paige asked Chloe.

"What are we, in sixth grade? No, I didn't tell," Chloe said.

"Then how?" Paige looked around the table at her friends.

"Wait. What did we know?" Maggie asked.

Alexis quickly scanned the café, then leaned in and whispered, "That Paige is L.C. Brooks."

"What? I didn't know," Maggie said.

Everyone was quiet while they watched her. Paige knew when Maggie finally caught on.

She gasped. "You based the catcher on my brother. I salivated over my brother?"

"Shhhhh!!" all the girls said.

They looked around as the café grew quiet. Paige loved her small town because folks genuinely cared about each other. Consequently, it was the worst thing about living in a small town —no privacy.

"Remember, ladies, L.C. Brooks's identity needs to be kept a secret until she reveals it at the signing," Alexis whispered.

Chloe leaned in. "Does Ethan know you're going to do the signing?"

"Yes. He knows." Paige beamed.

"Now that we have that news out of the way, I have to say, you're glowing," Chloe said.

Alexis crossed her arms, leaned back, and grinned. "You know, you really are. Do tell."

"If this involves my brother, I don't know if I want to know," Maggie said.

Alexis rolled her eyes.

Paige never could keep her emotions hidden, and she was absolutely giddy about spending more time with Ethan and moving back home. "I quit my job, and I have a plan to keep the bookstore open." She also knew how to steer a conversation in the direction she wanted it to go.

"You're staying?!" Maggie asked.

Paige nodded. "Yes. Deer Creek Falls is where I belong."

Chloe held up her glass of iced tea. "Damn right it is. Cheers!"

Paige's friends leaned in and said at the same time, "Tell us the plan."

She filled them in on how their items at the silent auction had brought in thousands of dollars for the charity.

"That's incredible," Maggie said.

"I placed a stack of business cards you all gave me by your items. They were gone by the end of the night. So, between the popularity of the items and at least one tourist a day asking where the souvenir shop had moved to, I decided that what the store needed was to stock gift items and commissioned works, too."

"I stopped in while you were gone and noticed a new display," Alexis said.

Paige told them about Lily taking over and arranging everything. They all laughed.

Their waitress brought their lunch orders. "Can I get you all anything else?"

"Everything looks delicious, thank you," Alexis said.

When the waitress walked away, Maggie said, "You could hold DIY classes in the back of the store."

"That's a great idea." Paige took a forkful of her strawberry-and-feta salad.

As Alexis squeezed the ketchup bottle to douse her fries, it sounded like she had sat on a whoopee cushion. Maggie broke into giggles.

"What are you, three?" Alexis rolled her eyes and continued with the conversation. "Maybe you could try for a liquor license and serve wine like they do at those painting classes in the cities."

"How would you know about paint and wine classes?" Maggie asked Alexis.

"I don't live under a rock." Alexis stuck out her tongue at Maggie.

"Who's acting like a three-year-old now?" Maggie laughed.

"I talked to Cole and Lily already," Paige said. "I have a few others to contact. I wondered, Maggie, if you'd like to sell your items, too?"

"I'd love that. I have a few signs that would be perfect for people's cabins, and I just finished a lamp fashioned from a couple of old oars."

"Great. I can't wait to see them."

As they ate lunch, Paige listened to her friends' ideas.

Chloe leaned in and whispered to Paige, "Don't think you can get away with changing the subject. I expect details."

Paige whispered to Chloe, "Sizzling," and popped one of Chloe's fries into her mouth.

PAIGE HURRIED TOWARD TURNER BOOKS. Her lunch with the girls had run late, and her door sign had promised a one-o'clock return. A sea of red, white, and blue adorned the streets. Colorful flower baskets hung from the old-fashioned light posts, and American flags hung from each business. Tourists strolled down Main Street, admiring window displays and walking in and out of shops with bags in hand.

She needed to call the artisans still on her list and get ready for the last festival committee meeting the following morning. As she unlocked the front door of the shop, her phone showed an incoming text from Ethan.

Hey beautiful.

How's your visit with Luke?

Good, but can't wait to see you. Talk tonight?

Yes! Miss you. Heart emoji.

PAIGE SHIFTED the grocery bag and reached into her purse for the house key. The lights were on inside, but the door was locked.

Weird. She opened it and called, "Hello! Grandpa, are you here?" Abe had transitioned to a cane and wasn't needing much care anymore.

"In here, sweet pea!"

"Sorry I'm late," Paige said as she followed his voice into the kitchen. "I picked up fixings for sandwiches if that's okay."

"Hi, honey."

"Oh, Elsie, I didn't know you were here. I hope you can join us for dinner. It's not much, I'm afraid." Paige set the bag of groceries on the counter and began putting away the sharp cheddar and roast beef.

"Sandwiches sound delightful. I believe I will."

Abe patted the chair next to him at the kitchen table. "Come sit."

Paige closed the fridge and looked to Elsie. Elsie nodded.

"Is everything okay?" Paige asked.

"Everything is fine. We want to talk, that's all," Elsie said.

"Okay, sure."

As Paige took a seat, Elsie placed a hand over Abe's. "Did you know that Abe and I were good friends when we were growing up? When we were sixteen, we agreed that if neither of us found someone by the time we were twenty-one, we'd marry each other."

"Really?"

Elsie nodded and smiled. "Your grandmother moved to town a few years later and your grandfather was smitten. I met Thomas soon after."

Abe interlaced his fingers with Elsie's. Paige looked back and forth between two of the dearest people in her life. "Are you two . . . ?"

They nodded. "We weren't sure how to tell you."

They all stood and hugged. "I'm so happy for you," Paige

said. "Wait, how did I not know this? Why wasn't it on Town Talk?"

Elsie shrugged. "I guess the gossip mill isn't interested in old people."

"I have something to tell you, too."

They looked at each other, then back to her, and smiled. "We know, dear."

"You know?"

"Of course. L.C.—Lincoln. Caroline. Brooks was your maternal grandmother's name."

Paige nodded. "When I realized the initials L and C, spoken together, formed the word Elsie, I knew I'd found the perfect pen name. I got to honor the three people I loved most in this world."

"You mean four people." Elsie winked.

"Yes. My hero turned out more like Ethan than I realized. You knew too, Grandpa?"

"I suspected when you sent me a list with your book suggestions. When I read it, I knew."

"You read *Catch Me*?" Paige was mortified.

"Of course. I read *Interception*, too, and I can't wait to read *Power Play*. I'm proud of you, Paige, and all you've accomplished. They're wonderful love stories."

"Will you forgive me for not telling you?" Paige asked.

"Nothing to forgive." Abe placed his hand on hers. "I hope you'll forgive me for not telling you about my relationship with Elsie—I wasn't sure how you'd feel about it. I loved your grandmother with my whole heart and now after all these years, I've fallen in love with this wonderful woman." He kissed Elsie on the cheek.

They made a cute couple, and both deserved to be happy again.

"I have more news, actually. I quit my job, I'm moving home, and I think I've found a way to keep the bookstore open."

"That's wonderful! I knew you'd find a way," Elsie said.

"This calls for a celebration." Abe stood, headed to the fridge, and took out a bottle of champagne.

Paige gathered glasses, then filled them in on her plans.

CHAPTER TWENTY-ONE

*A*be had warned her she'd have a hard time finding a place to park. Paige was lucky enough to find a spot in front of the Sampson brothers' Victorian home. She'd wanted to help at the store, but Elsie had insisted she not arrive until right before the signing.

The humidity had broken the night before, and a soft breeze from the lake helped to cool down the warm summer day. Food trucks lined both sides of Main Street. The savory scents of deep-fried cheese curds, cotton candy, and popcorn floated on the breeze. She waved to Rosie's niece, standing in front of her food truck as she carried on an animated conversation with the man in the neighboring American Legion roasted-corn stand. Music pumped from speakers set on the temporary stage in front of the Eagle's Nest. The street dance later that night would feature Roadhouse Romp, an up-and-coming country band.

People talked and laughed while browsing through the side-walk sales, and kids ran down the cordoned-off streets blowing bubbles and waving American flags.

The banner that stretched across the street announcing the

Fourth of July festival was the same one Paige remembered from her youth. She smiled, even though the butterflies in her stomach wanted to take flight. She quickened her pace. Was she ready? Paige inhaled deeply and opened the back door to Turner Books. She had a book signing to attend.

She paced behind the curtain as she waited for her name to be announced.

Chloe placed a hand on her shoulder. "Relax. You've got this. You've worked hard for it. Focus on making a grand entrance. Enjoy it."

Abe's voice rang loud and clear over the chatter on the other side of the curtain. "Thank you all for coming. Proceeds from each book sold today will be matched and donated to Project Night-Light, a charity near and dear to our author. Project Night-Light provides kids with a blanket, books, night-light, and a set of pajamas in a colorful tote bag." He held up the bag.

"Now without further ado, the moment you've all been waiting for, please welcome our very own Paige Turner, otherwise known as L.C. Brooks!"

Gasps and clapping greeted her as she came out from behind the curtain. She hugged her grandpa, placed a kiss on his soft, wrinkled cheek, and turned to face a packed room. "Wow. Thank you so much. I'm touched. Thank you."

She sat on a wooden stool and read a favorite part of her first book—a tender moment that had happened between the hero and heroine. The passage had been a favorite of Chloe's, one she couldn't stop talking about when she'd first read *Catch Me*. She finished her reading with the first chapter of *Power Play*, hoping to entice the audience to buy the book.

For the first time in her life, she felt free. Free from the secrets she'd worn like a weighted blanket. She'd worried keeping her identity secret would cause animosity, but those who knew her greeted her with love and affection. Even Missy listened intently as she read. She knew returning to Minnesota was the right decision. Family wasn't only those who shared DNA, but a community she could count on and who supported each other.

Paige closed the book and scanned the crowd. She and Ethan had exchanged texts and talked on the phone all week. He'd said he'd be back in time for the signing and there he was, standing in the back. He must have slipped in while she was reading. He winked. She couldn't wait to tell him she was staying in Deer Creek Falls. She stepped behind the table of books, pen in hand, and a line formed in front of her. She listened to her fans talking amongst themselves about the characters in her books and how some wished for their own happily ever after. Her grandpa told anyone who would listen about the remodeled space they'd be occupying at the end of the month, inviting them back for the grand reopening.

"I can't believe you're L.C. Brooks. I loved your first two books. I can't wait to read this one." Paige recognized Rachel, the mother of the adorable Levi. She frequented the bookstore regularly, always looking for a new mystery or romance and a pile of children's books. She hugged the book to her chest before she set it in front of Paige to sign.

"Thank you." Paige smiled and signed her name.

The line of people snaking out the front door and down the sidewalk astounded her. To think they were all there to see her.

"Hi, how are you?" Paige greeted each person and signed each book, occasionally adding a message. She tried to concentrate on the excited faces in front of her, but her thoughts always wandered back to Ethan. She thought of the day she'd walked into the bookstore and caught him singing to "Start Me Up."

A book was slid in front of her. "You can make it out to Ethan."

Paige looked up at the sound of Ethan's voice. He smiled his beautiful smile, with that sexy dimple and those laugh lines around his eyes.

The murmurs in the crowd increased. The energy rocketed around the room like an electric current.

She knew exactly what to write. "To Ethan Reynolds, the only man I have ever loved." She slid the book back to him.

"I took a job in New York so we can be together," Ethan said.

Oh no. Oh, how she loved this man. Paige bit down on her lip. "I quit my job in New York. I'm moving back to Deer Creek Falls." She waited for his reaction, but his smile remained intact.

Ethan leaned in, and the crowd and the noise seemed to vanish. He took her hand, pulled her out of the chair, and held her close. "I guess we should have talked about our future." He grinned.

Paige looked into his hazel eyes, bluer today as they reflected the short-sleeved blue Henley stretched across his broad chest. "This is my favorite place."

"Where? Deer Creek Falls?"

Paige snuggled close. "Nope. Right here in your arms. It doesn't matter where we are as long as you're with me."

Ethan kissed the top of her head, placed his hands in hers, and stepped back.

He lowered himself to one knee as he pulled a blue velvet box out of his pocket.

Paige's hand flew to her mouth and she looked down at him, stunned.

"Paige Turner. You are my sexy librarian and I love you with all my heart. I want to be there to catch you even if you don't need rescuing. I fell in love with you when you used your crazy ninja skills on me. I would love nothing more than to spend the rest of my life with you. Paige Turner, will you marry me?"

Choked up, she whispered, "Yes." She pulled him up, wrapped her arms around his neck, and kissed him. Cheers, clapping, and cameras flashing broke into their moment. They turned and smiled. Best day ever. She'd found her happily ever after. "You know this will be on the Town Talk app, right?"

"Good," Ethan answered. "News like this is worth spreading."

EPILOGUE

*M*ulti-colored bouquets of balloons swayed in the gentle breeze at the entrance of Turner Books, announcing their grand re-opening.

Maggie Reynolds held the door open for a group of customers as they streamed out with canvas totes in hand. After a quick detour home to check in a late-arriving guest, she was back at the store to help clean and restock the shelves and displays. She was relieved to have the money to pay this month's construction loan, but wished she had the time and money to renovate the last of the cabins.

With a deep breath she stepped into the swarm of customers. Maggie spotted Lily behind the counter. The two were becoming good friends, having found a common interest in design. "Hey, Lily. Have you decided what you're going to do with your scavenger-hunt winnings?"

The five-hundred-dollar prize was won by Lily and her mom, who was visiting from New York. With her eye for detail and inquisitive nature, it wasn't surprising how fast she'd solved the clues.

"I'm a tad boring. I put it into savings for my next plane ticket to visit Mom."

"Not boring at all. That's a great idea."

A customer set a few books on the counter, along with a "Gone Fishing" sign Maggie had painted on an old scrap of wood siding, so she left Lily to ring in the sale and made her way over to her grandma, Emma, and Rosie. They had their heads together and looked like they were up to something. No doubt match-making again. At least she was safe; she had a boyfriend.

"So, what are you three up to?"

Rosie jumped and placed a hand on her chest. "Good golly, child. You scared me."

Maggie rolled her eyes. Rosie, so dramatic. She guessed it was due to her theatre background.

Elsie placed a hand on Maggie's arm. "We were discussing this and that."

"Nice try. Who are you trying to set up now?"

Her great-aunt waved her off. "I plead the fifth," she joked.

"Well, at least Emma admits you've been up to no good." Maggie kissed her grandma on the cheek. "Carry on." Maggie walked over to Cole.

Cole nudged her. "I noticed a lot of your creations have sold."

"Yeah, who would've thought?"

He looked at her like she was crazy. "Are you kidding? Upcy-cling is the craze right now, and you're incredibly talented."

"Thank you." Maggie appreciated the way Cole, an artist himself, always had something nice to say. "I noticed the cutting boards in the kitchen section are gone."

"Yeah, I should have brought more." They both glanced around the store. "They have a good thing going here," Cole said.

"I agree. Paige had a great idea, allowing us creatives a place to sell our merchandise."

"Oh! I'll catch you later, Maggie." Cole rushed toward the door to help Ms. Johnston with her purchases.

Maggie loved her hometown. The way the townspeople came together to support Ethan and Paige warmed her heart. Everyone seemed to be enjoying themselves. Nikki and Nora were comfortable in the oversized beanbag chairs, reading a book in the kids' section. Abe chatted with Garrett, no doubt about beer, and Zeke flirted with a perky blonde.

Alexis stood by the rack of book-related T-shirts and held one up in front of her: *Boys in Books Are Better.* Maggie laughed and gave her a thumbs-up from across the store.

"Hey Maggie, did you get your guests settled?" Paige asked, joining her.

"I did. Nice couple." Maggie glanced around the room. "What a turnout, huh?"

"Yeah, can you believe it? We're really pleased. You outdid yourself. I can't believe I made my grandpa's wall of fame. The collage is beautiful. I do need to ask you something, though. Do you have a minute?"

"Sure."

She and Paige moved to the back of the store, away from the chatter.

"My brother looks happy. I'm glad you were able to reconnect. I'm happy for you two."

Paige side-hugged her. "Thanks, Maggie. I'm looking forward to having a sister."

"Me too." Maggie beamed.

"I would love if you'd be one of my bridesmaids."

Fleetingly, Maggie thought back to the bubble-gum engagement ring she'd worn for a few hours the previous year. She wrapped Paige in a hug. "I would love to. Thank you for asking. Have you set a date?"

Ethan peeked around the corner with a large grin on his face. "The sooner the better."

Paige laughed. "We haven't settled on a date yet."

ROSIE and the elder twins listened from a table nearby. "We hit it out of the park, ladies. I knew our plan would work." Rosie took a sip of her iced coffee and looked to her childhood friends.

"We did good," Elsie said.

Abe came up behind Elsie and placed a hand on her shoulder. "Hey now, you ladies can't take all the credit. I did get her here!"

Elsie patted his hand. "Yes honey, you did play a part."

"So, who's next?" Emma asked.

At the same time, Rosie and Elsie said, "Maggie!"

Abe shook his head and placed a gentle kiss on Elsie's cheek. "I'll leave you three to your scheming."

"What about Zeke?" Emma asked.

Elsie watched Zeke flirt with yet another woman. "Zeke's not ready. Besides, Maggie has been a bridesmaid too many times. It's time she gets her turn at being a bride."

Rosie nodded. "You're right, Elsie, it's time to marry off Maggie. I'm just not sure Jared is her soul mate."

The twins nodded in agreement. "And that is why we have our work cut out for us," Elsie said.

ABOUT THE AUTHOR

Ellie Rhodes is an identical twin author duo who write *sweet with a little heat,* small-town romance novels. They love writing about strong, independent, fun, and flirty women and swoon-worthy men who make them laugh (they hope they make you laugh too!) They both have husbands who are their real-life heroes and who put up with, what their husbands refer to as, their "twin speak" (never endless mind-reading looks and bursts of uncontrollable laughter). When they aren't writing, both can completely lose track of time reading a good book and enjoy their summers outside after being holed-up over the long winter months.

www.ellie-rhodes.com
facebook.com/ellie.rhodes.718689
instagram.com/author_ellie_rhodes

DEAR READER

Want to read a free short story?
Sign up for our newsletter today!
https://www.ellie-rhodes.com/newsletter

*Subscribers will be the first to learn when
the next book in the series will be released.*

Did you enjoy *Catch Me*?
Please visit the retailer's product page
if you enjoyed this story to leave a review.

Honest reviews of our books help
bring them to the attention of other readers.
We would be grateful if you could
spend a few minutes leaving a review.
Thank you!

Feel free to drop us a line.
Interacting with our readers is a highlight of our day,
I promise you'll get a reply, and I promise it will be from us.

Made in the USA
Monee, IL
07 July 2021